"People know about your son? Is it in the papers?"

"Not yet, but it will be. And you're so surprised, aren't you?" he sneered.

"You don't think that I…" Lindy said in a strangled voice. "Sam, I didn't…"

"Look me in the eyes and tell me that it wasn't you." He dragged his hand heavily through his hair. "Did you really think I kept silent about my son out of choice? Don't you think I'd have loved to boast about him?"

Lindy swallowed the lump of emotion in her throat. "I'm so sorry, Sam. But I can't be the only person who knows," she said desperately.

"You're the only one I don't trust."

Wanted: three husbands for three sisters!

Anna, Lindy and Hope—triplet sisters and the best, the closest, of friends. Physically, these three women may look alike, but their personalities are very different! Anna is lively and vivacious, Lindy is the practical one and Hope sparkles with style and sophistication.

But they have one thing in common: each sister is about to meet a man she will tantalize, torment and finally tame! And when these spirited women find true love, they'll become the most beautiful triplet brides....

Turn the page to enjoy Lindy's story in
The Secret Father

And look out for Hope in:
An Innocent Affair Harlequin Presents® #2114

Kim Lawrence

THE SECRET FATHER

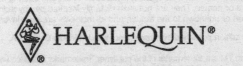

HARLEQUIN®

TORONTO • NEW YORK • LONDON
AMSTERDAM • PARIS • SYDNEY • HAMBURG
STOCKHOLM • ATHENS • TOKYO • MILAN • MADRID
PRAGUE • WARSAW • BUDAPEST • AUCKLAND

ISBN 0-373-12096-6

THE SECRET FATHER

First North American Publication 2000.

CHAPTER ONE

SAM ROURKE scanned the diners in the small restaurant. He recognised and exchanged nods with several members of the film crew relaxing over their food. There were three women sitting alone, and none of them bore any resemblance to the divine Lacey, but then that would have been too much to hope for.

He spoke softly to the proprietor, who had materialised as if by magic at his side, and discovered that the woman he was looking for was the only one of the three solitary females not looking at him. In fact she was probably the only person in the entire room—other than the crew members, in whom familiarity had bred a healthy contempt—not looking at him. Sam was too accustomed to attention to do more than subconsciously register the scrutiny.

He had to know every eye in the place was fixed on him, Lindy thought scornfully. She deliberately directed her own blue-eyed stare elsewhere. He positively struts, she decided, furtively taking in the long-legged lope. Her lips twisted in a small derisive smile as she twirled the stem of her frosted glass between her long, shapely fingers. He was lapping it up! She glanced at her watch and frowned; Hope was late, but then her sister's unpunctuality was legendary.

'Dr Lacey?'

Lindy started and found herself looking directly up into the face of Sam Rourke. Like most of the civilised world she'd seen his face in close up, enlarged to godlike proportions on the silver screen. A realist, she was quite prepared for a disappointment: make-up, lighting and a

5

lot of hype could transform the most ordinary of crea-
tures.

Sam Rourke was by no stretch of the imagination ordinary! In the flesh, the heavy-lidded eyes were just as
startlingly sapphire-blue, the mobile lips just as sensually
sculpted and the jawline just as square. His dark wavy
hair was brushed back from the trademark widow's peak
and the cleft in his chin deepened as he met her critical
stare.

'Mr Rourke,' she said, as though she were well used
to meeting international superstars over her lunch. She
was disgusted to find her nervous system had gone into
instant shock when exposed to the undoubtedly high-
octane charisma this man oozed. Happily this state of
affairs did not show on her calm features. Her delicate
colour didn't fluctuate even a little as she smiled dis-
tantly.

'Hope couldn't make it.' Without waiting to be in-
vited, he took the seat opposite her. 'She asked me to
meet you and show you the way to the house.'

So, Sam Rourke knew the way to her sister's house.
How cosy. Lindy couldn't help speculating just how well
Hope, who was professionally known by her surname,
Lacey, knew this man. She'd volunteered nothing about
him beyond the basic fact that he was her director and
co-star in the film they'd been shooting for the past two
months here in Maine.

Lindy didn't know whether to read anything into this
unusual circumstance. Hope had a wicked tongue and
usually she delighted in telling her sisters how disappointing the famous people she'd met were in real life.
Perhaps she hadn't found Sam Rourke disappointing.
They would certainly make a striking pair, her beautiful
sister and this man, and it was almost *de rigueur* for
supermodels to be squired by actors or rock stars.

It wouldn't do either of their careers any harm to be

seen together. Lindy stifled this cynical and uncharitable thought. She might be a supermodel, but her sister Hope was curiously untouched by the more unpleasant aspects of the world she moved in; she was as warm and genuine as she had been the day she'd left their English village home.

'I wouldn't like to impose,' she began firmly, not at all happy about the prospect of sharing her table with this larger-than-life individual. She'd made the mistake once of being seduced by a pretty face and these days it took more than a sinfully attractive smile to win her approval. If she was honest, men blessed in the looks department, at least this obviously, had to work extra hard to win her trust.

'Then I'll hint if you do,' her companion replied swiftly, an expression of boredom that made her wince beginning to spread across his features. When people went to these sorts of lengths to treat him normally the conversation frequently became monosyllabic. 'Have you ordered?' He flicked a cursory glance at the menu. 'The lobster's great here, isn't it, Albert?' The *maître d'* had materialised at his elbow. 'We'll have two.'

'I'm allergic to shellfish.'

'You're not!' He hit his forehead with the back of his hand and gestured to the waiter.

'No, I'm not,' she agreed sweetly. This man's casual, bored attitude and the fact he had taken her co-operation for granted made her normally placid blood quietly simmer. 'But I could be for all you know. I don't recall asking you to eat with me. I don't recall asking you to sit down.'

The famous blue eyes narrowed and he looked at her as if noticing her for the first time. English rose, Hope Lacey had said. No hothouse bloom certainly, but one of those pale pink, delicate things that grew in hedgerows. Good-looking in a style he'd always found some-

what colourless and bland. Nothing about her clothes or
demeanour was intended to catch the eye, but she had a
good figure from what he could see, and her bone structure was excellent. Her neck was singularly beautiful—
long and graceful. He appreciatively let his eyes dwell
on the slender curve for a moment.

'I'm not big on formalities.'

'I am,' she said in a calm, unflustered way. 'It saves
confusion.' I should have kept my mouth shut, she
thought regretfully. She hadn't much wanted to earn herself that rather cool appraisal from those famous blue
eyes, but it really did irritate her the way he'd breezed
in and taken over, all cool confidence and superficial
charm. He was no doubt confident that his blatant sexi-
ness would reduce any female with a pulse to a com-
pliant idiot.

'Shall we start again? I'm Sam Rourke and Hope
asked me to meet you.' For Hope's sake he tried to keep
his growing irritation from his voice. He didn't think
he'd done anything yet to justify this sort of antagonism.

'I know who you are, Mr Rourke,' Lindy said crisply.
'As does everyone in the room. To be quite frank, this
much curiosity would be disastrous for my digestion.'

It wouldn't do his own much good either, he reflected
wryly, but that obviously hadn't occurred to this woman.
If he'd planned to dine here, he'd have been seated in
the small secluded alcove that gave him some degree of
privacy. It was pretty obvious that his companion held
the firm belief that he thrived in being the centre of
attention. What the hell? Why disappoint the lady?

Sam turned his head with slow deliberation and gave
a dazzling smile to a group of elderly ladies at the next
table; they giggled like teenagers. Rick, a member of the
crew who had worked with Sam on several occasions,
witnessed the action from the opposite side of the room
and spilled his soup down his trousers. Sam intercepted

the amazed expression on the young man's face and deliberately winked.

Rick blotted the damp patch on his denims and wondered what on earth Sam was up to. Despite the public perception of the man, Sam Rourke was a disarmingly modest and amazingly self-effacing guy in private. On numerous occasions he'd seen him go to some lengths to avoid the attentions of his legions of drooling fans.

The expression in Sam's eyes as he returned his attention to Lindy was cynical. 'You worry when they don't notice you.' He could see from the look of disgust in her eyes that the doctor felt a lot better having her suspicions confirmed. Why not give an audience what it wanted?

Lindy gave a fractional shrug; she had no idea that she'd witnessed anything out of the ordinary. 'Just give me directions to the house and I'll leave you to eat your lunch in peace. Hold on a moment, I've got a notebook in my bag,' she said briskly, reaching for her leather shoulder-bag.

Sam leant back in his chair, his lips curving in a sardonic smile. 'Do you have a problem?' he drawled slowly.

'Pardon...?' she said, giving a reasonable impression of incomprehension. Was this the actor's ego, she wondered scornfully, that needed to be universally worshipped? Was she supposed to stare at him with slavish devotion?

'I'm just wondering whether to take this personally. Or do you freeze everyone at ten paces?'

Personally, she thought, maintaining a neutral expression. 'I'll ask for your autograph if that will help your anxiety attack,' she offered helpfully. Heavens, she thought in alarm, why on earth did I say that? Isn't it my role in life to apply soothing oil to troubled waters? Since when did I instigate hostility?

'Now English reserve I can tolerate, Doctor, but that
was plain nasty. Listen, I get the message, you don't like
me, but I gave my word to your sister that I'd see you
safely to her place. I'm not about to give you directions,
so the only way of finding the house is to stick with me.
I suggest you put a brave face on it, honey.'

The easy endearment and the edge of mockery in his
voice made her angry. 'I'm not hungry,' she insisted,
ignoring the growling of her stomach.

'You've just driven all the way from Boston; did I get
that much right?' He inclined his head as she nodded.
'Then you need to eat; *I* need to eat. Logic sort of makes
a pretty compelling case for us eating together.'

Put that way it was easy to see why he thought she
was making a fuss about nothing. No doubt the average
female would think finding herself dining with Sam
Rourke was as good as winning the lottery. I *am* making
a fuss about nothing, she thought, giving him a conces-
sionary but tepid smile.

The lobster was, in fact, just as delicious as he had
suggested and the portion so generous she couldn't finish
it. She pushed her plate away with a sigh. 'I'm stuffed,'
she said with rueful honesty.

Sam gave a sudden laugh and the sound made heads
turn, a fact he seemed oblivious of. 'You sounded so
like Hope,' he explained as she looked questioningly at
him.

'We *are* sisters.'

'It'd be easy to miss that.'

'She is beautiful,' Lindy agreed, without any trace of
jealousy that her companion could detect. Lindy knew
that she was hardly ugly, but competing with her sister
was not something she'd ever considered. The Lacey
triplets were as dissimilar in looks as they were in personality.

'I wasn't talking about physical similarity, or lack of it. I mean Hope is so warm and spontaneous...open.'

'I don't make a habit of gushing with total strangers, Mr Rourke,' she said, her smile fading. Why not just call me a cold fish and be done with it? she thought indignantly.

'You don't even trickle, Dr Lacey,' Sam Rourke commented drily. 'But then, as I'm sure you're going to point out, that is none of my business. I'm here to act as guide.' He couldn't have made it plainer that the whole thing had become something of a chore to him.

'I'm sorry I'm not a scintillating dining companion,' she observed waspishly. His criticism shouldn't have mattered to her, but inexplicably it hurt.

'I don't often get this sort of antagonism from women,' he remarked, leaning back in his chair and regarding her thoughtfully.

I just bet you don't, she thought, her scorn reflected in the light blue depths of her almond-shaped eyes.

'Guys, sure. "I never watch *your* sort of movie", is quite a common line. Then there's the other sort who want to show I'm not such a tough guy off the screen...'

'And are you?'

'A flicker of interest?' he mocked. 'What happened to the "I'm totally unimpressed by the fact you're a big star"?' He watched the faintest of flushes mount the smooth contours of her cheeks as his words found their mark. 'To answer your question, I'm not into bar brawls, not even to impress a lady. Besides,' he said, running a hand down the side of his jaw, 'I couldn't risk the face.' The languid self-mockery in his tone made her look sharply into his densely blue eyes. She averted her gaze as swiftly as she could; he had the most extraordinarily penetrating stare.

'I suppose it's an occupational hazard, people confus-

ing you with the characters you play. Even when
they're…'

'Go on,' he encouraged as she stopped abruptly, looking uncomfortable.

'Even when they're as two-dimensional and stereo-
typed as the ones you play.' She lifted her chin and tried
not to feel guilty for being so brutal. He had asked!

Sam sucked in his breath behind a display of even
white teeth and looked a long way from being mortally
wounded. 'Ouch!' he said, the last remnants of boredom
vanishing from his expression. 'Aren't *you* guilty of
judging me by the type of character I portray on the
screen? You know, the one who snaps his fingers and
has a tall, leggy blonde on his arm…' He ought to feel
guilty for winding her up, but it was irresistible.

'In his bed, usually,' she responded with a reluctant
smile, recalling the last film she'd seen him in; seen
quite a lot of him as she recalled. It was hard to look at
his chest and not remember how well muscled those
broad shoulders were. Then don't look at his chest, she
told herself crossly.

'You admit it, then?'

Lindy lifted her slender shoulders fractionally and
pursed her lips ruefully. Now that he'd said it, she
couldn't deny that her own instinctively aggressive reaction to him had been partially directed at the type of
macho wonder man he generally played. Big-box-office
roles, but not exactly stretching; that summed up Sam
Rourke's career.

'It could be I'm a great actor,' he suggested. 'I can
see you find that hard to believe.' He gave a long-
suffering sigh.

The lopsided smile was impossible not to respond to.
'Do you mean you won't act like an egocentric, narcis-
sistic, shallow—?'

'Now don't go expecting miracles. I never make

promises I can't keep,' he interrupted, holding up his hands to stem the flow. 'I have unplumbed shallows. Shall we just say I won't call you babe? It'll be hard, but I'm a very amenable guy deep down.'

'That's a weight off my mind,' she assured him solemnly, with an answering glimmer in her eyes. She'd seen Sam Rourke do humour, but that had been scripted. This dry, caustic wit was obviously the natural variety and she found it much more attractive than the slick, predictable banter.

It was gradually becoming obvious that, whilst the characters this man portrayed might arguably be two-dimensional, he was much more complex in the flesh. And distressingly perfect flesh it was too, she thought, pulling her glance from the sinewed strength of his fore-arms meshed with a fine covering of dark hair.

'Better, Doctor, much better,' he approved caustically. 'You know, you've got to learn to relax around us glittering, famous types if you're going to be part of the team.'

'I suppose I will,' she agreed doubtfully.

The offer of a job as medical advisor on the set of the film her sister was starring in had seemed like a heaven-sent opportunity. The doctor they'd had lined up had broken his leg and was in traction. They hadn't begun shooting any of the scenes with medical content yet, Hope had assured her. It would be a breeze! Lindy had just resigned from her job as a senior house officer at a prestigious London hospital and had needed time to sort out where she was going from there. Now she was here, Lindy was beginning to regret the impulsiveness of her actions.

'Won't people resent the fact I got the job because I'm Hope's sister?' What am I doing here? she wondered, feeling suddenly very homesick.

'Nepotism is one of the more savoury ways people get jobs in this business,' Sam observed drily.

'You're not telling me the casting couch still exists, are you?' she laughed.

'Such sweet innocence,' he mocked lightly. 'I was thinking more along the lines of murder, extortion, blackmail; but the old-fashioned ways are still the best, or so I'm told.'

Looking doubtfully into his cynical blue eyes, she wasn't sure whether he was joking. 'It all seems very casual,' she admitted.

Getting a job to her had entailed gruelling interviews and hard-won references, but here she was being offered a salary that made her blink, to do something which didn't sound very strenuous.

'I just got a phone call and a first-class ticket for Boston,' she said.

'Don't look so worried,' he advised with an amused smile. 'I'll make you work for your money. I'd assumed you were star-struck. Don't explode!' He raised a pacific hand. 'But, that obviously not being the case, it must be a man that made you up sticks.'

'A man?' she enquired with discouraging hauteur. It occurred somewhat belatedly to her that Sam Rourke was her new boss and it might have been politic to take that into account before she'd started sniping at him. She might just regret her honesty in the near future.

'Broken heart, love affair, that sort of thing. Though you don't look the type to...' Sam paused, weighing his words. Telling a woman, even one as self-contained as this one, that she didn't look as if she had enough fire in her veins might not go down too well.

'Make a fool of myself over a man?'

'My thought exactly,' he agreed with some relief.

'I'm not,' she said flatly. She had no intention of going over her reasons for leaving a job she'd loved. A man had certainly been involved—and love, too, if Simon Morgan was to be believed.

From the moment he'd taken over as consultant ortho-paedic surgeon, he'd made his personal interest in his house officer obvious. He hadn't got encouragement, but he hadn't needed it. He was one of that breed of men to whom things had always come easily, and he hadn't thought Rosalind Lacey was any different from anything else he'd wanted.

At first he'd taken her rejection to be part of a game—a game he was happy to play. When he'd dis-covered he'd been playing alone, things had got ugly and he'd made it quite obvious that the hospital wasn't big enough for both of them. She could have fought—should have fought—but Lindy hadn't had the stomach for a messy sexual harassment suit, which could have damaged her professional reputation even if she had won. America had been her way out of a classic catch-22 situation.

'I admire confidence,' Sam said softly.

The sceptical note in his voice, of a man who believed no woman was as invulnerable as she professed to be, irritated Lindy.

'Shouldn't we be making a move?' she said, looking around the now half-empty room.

'See you in the morning, Sam.' Rick, who was a thin, gangling youth with a shock of carrot-red hair, chose that moment to make his exit via their table. He eyed Lindy curiously.

'The new medico, Rick,' Sam said in answer to the silent enquiry.

'Pleased to meet you.' A friendly smile beamed out as he sketched a bow and saluted her flamboyantly. 'Don't keep Sam up too late,' he added over his shoul-der. 'Early start tomorrow, chief.'

'An actor?' Lindy asked.

'Crew.'

'He didn't think we…you and I were together?' she asked uncomfortably.

'I shouldn't think so,' Sam said, signing the cheque as he rose from the table. 'You're not my type.'

'How cruel of you to dash my girlish fantasies,' she responded, taking a bracing breath to weather this casual insult and following him towards the door. He could certainly give as good as he got.

'You should have locked the trunk,' Sam remonstrated a few minutes later as he lifted her cases from the rental car in which she'd driven to Maine.

'What do you think you're doing?' she asked sharply as he proceeded to place her luggage in the four-wheel drive parked next to her own car.

'The studio's arranged a car for you; it's at the house. The hire firm are picking this one up.' He got into his car and glanced pointedly at his watch.

Lindy swallowed this information and climbed up into the passenger seat beside him. After they'd been driving for a few minutes she asked, 'Is it far?'

'About twenty minutes.' He turned off the highway onto a narrow, uneven dirt road. 'Hope's found a gem of a place.'

'She said it's right by the sea.' Lindy tried to resurrect the optimism and anticipation she'd initially felt when she'd embarked on this adventure.

'Owl Cove,' Sam said.

'Will she be working late?'

Sam flicked her a sideways glance. 'There is no shooting today.'

'But I thought you said…'

'I said she couldn't make it. I didn't say why.'

There was some indefinable note in his voice that bothered Lindy. 'Well, say why now, or is it some secret?'

'Not the best kept secret in the world.'

'Meaning?' she said, with an edge in her voice reserved for people who bad-mouthed either of her sisters.

'Forget it,' Sam advised, shrugging his shoulders.

'It's a bit late for that. Has something happened to Hope…?'

Her hands—well kept, rather lovely hands, he noticed—fluttered as the note of anxiety crept into her voice. He noticed the gesture because all her movements up to that point had been very precise and controlled, just like the lady herself.

'Nothing like that,' he soothed swiftly. 'The word is that Lloyd Elliot and Hope are an item.'

Lindy relaxed; so Hope was in love. 'Well, I know he's older than her…' It had been a good ten years since Lloyd Elliot had starred in a film, but as a producer and director with half a dozen box-office hits under his belt his name was still very much public property.

'And married—very married.'

Lindy went pale. 'Hope wouldn't have an affair with a married man.'

'If you say so.'

'I *do* say so!' she rapped, glaring at his smug profile. 'My sisters would never get involved with married men.'

'I almost forgot, Hope did say you're triplets,' he said, half to himself. 'This sort of thing does happen on film sets, you know. On average I'd say we see a divorce and a handful of illicit romances. It's a very claustrophobic environment and film-set flings are not that unusual. It's no big deal.

'Here we are,' he said soon after, swinging the car into a driveway that led to a white clapper-board, single-storey building surrounded by a deck that had a view of the rocky and secluded bay. The view was only enjoyed by a scattering of homes that lay clustered on the tree-covered slopes.

Any other time Lindy would have been enchanted by the place, but as she clambered from the high vehicle she was trembling with indignation and shock. That he could accuse her sister and then have the absolute gall to make an affair with a married man sound—how had he put it?—'no big deal'!

His broad back was turned to her as he proceeded to pull her luggage from the back. 'How dare you tar my sister with the same brush as yourself?'

The low intensity of her tone made Sam spin around. For a moment he was too stunned by the sudden change from calm serenity to ferocious anger to reply. He'd never been a contributor to the theory that cool women had an untapped core of fire, and he'd certainly never felt the urge to prove the case one way or the other.

Still waters looked a lot more interesting than he'd have thought possible. Sam ruthlessly extinguished the spark of interest. He couldn't afford to explore any possibilities right now, at a time when his energies were totally committed to the task ahead. He didn't need distractions; this was his first time out wearing the director's cap and his role was a million miles away from the familiar format the public knew and loved.

He was charged up at the prospect of the months' work ahead. Besides, this woman hadn't even tried to hide the fact that she looked on him as a piece of beef cake and nothing else. It was something he was accustomed to, but her attitude really riled him. For some obscure reason he wanted to be around when Rosalind Lacey was forced to accept that he was more than a pretty face.

'You asked, and I told you how it looks. They're not being exactly discreet if you must know. If you want to believe your sister is as pure as the driven snow, that's fine by me. I didn't set out to bad-mouth either of them, but you're bound to hear a lot cruder speculation before

long,' Sam warned her. 'More to the point, so is Lloyd's
wife. You do *know* he's married to Dallas?' he said, with
a hint of incredulity that anyone could be ignorant of
this fact. The couple had a very well-documented relationship.

'She's a singer, isn't she?' Her summer-blue eyes had
grown stormily grey as she glared angrily at him, and
her angular jaw was set at an aggressive angle.

Sam shook his head incredulously. 'You could say
that,' he agreed mockingly. 'Dynamite Dallas, they call
her, and when she hears of this little escapade I should
think she'll live up to her name.' It occurred to him that
this quiet, subdued creature could give even the tempes-
tuous Dallas a run for her money when she lost her temper.

'I don't give a damn what they call her,' Lindy
snapped. 'But if I hear anyone maligning my sister
they'll have me to answer to.'

Sam let out a soundless whistle as she stalked up to
the front door, unwittingly giving him a view of her
excellent rear in a close-fitting linen skirt. 'Yes, ma'am,'
he breathed, amused laughter rumbling in his chest as
he tucked one case under his arm and followed her.

Inside, the house was much bigger than it had appeared. Pale walls, lots of exposed stone and gleaming
wood floors scattered with vibrant rugs all conspired to
cool her temper. The trembling that afflicted her limbs
had subsided by the time she arrived at the Jacuzzi that
was built into a covered deck overlooking a sandy horse-
shoe sweep and the sea beyond.

'This is incredible.'

'It is, isn't it?' a soft voice at her elbow agreed.

'You scared me half to death!' she accused, spinning
around. She was already deeply regretting losing her
temper in front of this man. Over the years she'd grown
very adept at hiding her innermost feelings. The ability

gave her an illusion of security. Suddenly she felt more
vulnerable than she had done in years. Even the hateful
Simon hadn't succeeded in making her lose her dignity.
'I thought you'd gone.'

'As you see, I haven't.' His gaze was fixed on the
distant horizon with an odd expression of longing.

'Don't let me keep you.'

'I thought I'd have a shower.'

Lindy blinked. 'You thought *what*?'

He stretched lazily, extending his back, making cir-
cular motions with his shoulders. The fabric of his shirt
pulled taut, making Lindy conscious of the strength in
his powerful body.

'Shower,' he elucidated helpfully. 'It's been a long
day.'

'You can't...' She was pretty certain that her sister's
hospitality didn't extend this far; her own certainly
didn't. As far as Lindy was concerned, the sooner this
man left her in peace the better! Her eyes widened as
he calmly began unbuttoning his shirt. To her relief—
damn it, she *was* relieved—he stopped halfway.

'Didn't Hope mention it? I'm her house guest.'

Lindy froze as, whistling, he casually strolled from
the room. It couldn't be true, she told herself. Share a
roof with that wretched man—no way! Her total rejection of the idea left no room for mental negotiation of
the situation. Heart pumping out adrenaline, she strode
after him and pushed open the door from behind which
she could hear sounds of activity.

'I'm not staying here...' she began hotly, barging into
the room.

'My bathroom in particular, or this house?' he enquired with a deadpan expression. He didn't appear in
the least put out that he was standing there clad only in
a pair of black boxer shorts. He kicked the trousers that
lay at his feet to one side.

Lindy made a last-ditch attempt to recapture some of her legendary cool and failed miserably. She was staring, her eyes travelling upwards from his feet. She knew it, but was helpless to do anything else. He stretched up to switch on the shower and the muscles in his torso rippled.

On screen she'd seen he had a sexy, beautiful body, but the intimacy of a cinema was illusionary. In the flesh, quite literally, the basic earthiness of his appeal made a physical impact. From the spasm in her stomach and her dry, tight throat to the heavy, leaden sensation in her uncooperative limbs, she was transfixed by the spectacle.

'Have you seen enough, or are you planning on joining me?' The satiny quality of his deep voice had never been more apparent. 'You do look as if you could do with cooling down,' he observed. 'If we're going to be sharing a roof perhaps we should get the ground rules sorted out up front. It gives a guy a certain feeling of insecurity when even his bathroom isn't private. I've had to deal with some determined fans in my time, but this is a first!'

It was the taunting quality in his voice that did it, made her react so childishly. The 'you're no different from all the others' tone that made her hackles rise— and the disturbing possibility that there was the merest grain of truth in his words. The sponge was lying on the edge of the washbasin; she picked it up and lobbed it at his smirking face. Her aim was spot on: the saturated missile landed square in his face.

She wasn't quite sure which one of them was more surprised by her action, but Sam was the first to recover. 'Maybe this will cool you down.' He redirected the angle of the shower head towards her and she let out a shriek as the water hit her. Blinded by the water, she closed her eyes and reached out blindly for a towel.

The grunt of pain came after she collided with a solid

object. Out of the direct line of fire she wiped her face on the sleeve of her silk blouse. 'Of all the stupid things,' she squeaked. 'Turn that thing off!'

It was at that point she saw the blood, drops of it on the tiled floor. Medically speaking, she knew that a little blood could look like a lot, but from a more personal viewpoint the sight made her stomach lurch. It wasn't much more comforting when she looked at Sam. He was leaning against the wall, his hand raised to his nose, from which a steady flow of blood was seeping. He looked more bemused than distressed.

'How...?'

'You head-butted me,' he informed her.

'I didn't mean...' she began, her eyes widening in dismay. 'I couldn't see what I was doing.'

'Hope mentioned nothing about homicidal tendencies. I seem to recall "quiet" was mentioned, and "needs bringing out of herself" featured somewhere in there.'

'I feel guilty enough as it is,' she said from between clenched teeth.

'Good,' he replied, his voice muffled by his hand.

She completed the job he'd begun and got completely drenched as she reached in the shower cubicle and turned off the water. 'Let me see,' she said, adopting a professional tone. She'd probably never felt less professional in her entire life, but now wasn't the moment to ponder that circumstance. 'I am a doctor.'

'Trade can't be so bad you have to go out assaulting innocent bystanders.'

'You are not innocent,' she said feelingly. 'It doesn't look too bad,' she observed with some relief. 'Hold it here, like so.' She took his thumb and forefinger and demonstrated on her own nose where he should apply the pressure. 'Not on me,' she said, frustrated by his flippant attitude. She removed his fingers from her own small straight nose. 'We could do with some ice and a first-aid kit.'

'Speak for yourself. I could do with a drink; I'm in shock.'

'If you were, which you're not,' she said, eyeing his healthy colour with a certain degree of resentment, 'the last thing you'd need would be alcohol.'

'Hope has a first-aid kit in the kitchen and the refrigerator's there, too.'

Leaving a trail of wet footprints behind her, Lindy made her way to the galley kitchen which was divided from the living area by a peninsula of fitted cupboards.

'Top cupboard on the right,' said Sam, who had followed her.

'Don't release the pressure; you're dripping everywhere,' she censured.

'Yes, Doctor,' he said meekly.

Lindy gave him a sharp look; he was giving the impression of someone who was *enjoying* himself, which, unless he was seriously abnormal, couldn't be the case!

She pulled out a stool, slipped off her sodden shoes and, hitching up her pencil skirt, climbed up to reach the cupboard. She turned around and found that Sam was taking full advantage of his clear view of her legs.

'Disgusting!' she said, and received an unrepentant grin.

She climbed down again. 'Sit down; I can't reach,' she said brusquely. Sam complied and with gauze she cleaned the blood from his face, trying not to meet his eyes as she did so; it wasn't easy. The skin didn't look discoloured and she told him there probably wouldn't be any bruising.

'Lloyd will be—hell, can I let go now?' He'd seen her lips twitch as his sexy drawl was reduced to an adenoidal mumble.

'I think so,' she agreed as the flow seemed to have been staunched.

'As I was saying, Lloyd will be pleased. Me being unable to film could cost the production megabucks.'

'I didn't think of that,' she said guiltily.

'Before you viciously assaulted me.'

Lindy drew in an indignant breath. 'You're right,' she said, slowly releasing it. 'You *are* a good actor. Seriously, it was an accident. What is it now?' she asked as he closed one eye, opened it and gave a deep sigh.

'There's something I think you should know...'

'Well?'

'Your shirt's totally transparent when it's wet.'

A moment's blank incomprehension and then horror spread across her face as one glance down confirmed his statement. Why, today of all days, had she not worn a bra?

Solicitously he offered her a tea-towel. 'This might cover the...er...dilemma.'

Glaring at him, she snatched at the lifeline. 'You took your time to mention it.'

'Would you believe I didn't notice? No, I thought not. It took my mind off the pain.' He leant his head back against the wall and gave an appreciative sigh. 'You really have a *great* body.'

'How dare...?'

'Now don't go all double standards on me, Doctor. You weren't exactly displaying professional interest in my body back there. Don't get embarrassed about it—I'm used to being treated like a sex object. Your mouth's open,' he observed gently, reaching forward to tilt her jaw upwards. 'I was only making an honest evaluation. I have to say I thought I was pretty good at summing people up, but I was quite wrong with you. I know this is clichéd, but you really should get mad more often.'

'Well, really,' she said weakly. She knew sexual

chemistry when she felt it; she'd felt it before with disastrous consequences. That fact alone ought to have made it easy to laugh away his glib nonsense. He was an actor; deceit was second nature to him; she had to get out of this situation—fast!

'You hide behind that cool, classy exterior, but I don't believe it any more, so why pretend? I much prefer you uncoordinated and clumsy—more human. You don't need props.' His voice was soothingly seductive as he pulled away the towel clutched to her bosom. 'That's a start.' The unconfined sway of her breasts made his breath come faster.

Heat crawled over her skin where his eyes touched—caressed. 'You should put some ice on your nose,' she said, desperation creeping into her voice as, simultaneously, paralysis crept into her limbs.

It was a blur to her, but somehow she had straddled his lap, her skirt riding indecently high against her thighs, and her face was being held firmly between his hands. His lips were firm, cool and unalarming. With a small cry her arms went around his neck and she stopped being passive. It was as if he'd tapped into a source she hadn't known was there—an elemental, fiery core.

It was Sam's turn to look startled when they broke apart. 'Wow!' His flippancy didn't have the ring of authenticity about it.

'Lindy, we're home!' The lilting sound of her sister's voice rang out as the kitchen door was flung open.

'Timing is everything,' Sam muttered under his breath.

'I see you've met Sam.' Dry as dust, Hope's voice cut through the startled silence.

I'll strangle her, Lindy decided. After I drown myself, she added silently. She glanced resentfully at the floor which still hadn't opened up and swallowed her.

Hope and the man beside her slowly took in the scene

before them and to Lindy it seemed to take them for
ever. With each agonising second her feelings of self-
disgust grew.

'Nice afternoon, you two?' Sam said, his tone betray-
ing no evidence of discomfort.

'Not as interesting as yours.' The expression in the
older man's eyes made Lindy cringe inside. Her face
froze and her spine straightened to attention. She slid off
Sam's knee, stopping his objection with one cold glance.

'There was an accident,' she said. I sound normal, she
realised with amazement. 'Mr Rourke...'

Sam snorted at her formality. 'Dr Lacey,' he said sardonically, 'butted me in the face. Busted my nose.'

The humour faded dramatically from Lloyd's face.
For the first time he seemed to notice the evidence of
bloodstains. 'Hell-fire, Sam, have you any idea how
much over budget we could be if you mess up your
face?' he demanded hotly. 'The insurance premiums we
pay because you insist on doing those damned stunts are
astronomical as it is.'

Sam shot Lindy an ironic look before he replied. 'The
doctor assures me my beauty is undimmed.'

'I can see a damned bruise. I swear I can,' Lloyd
insisted. 'Put some ice on it, Sam,' he said, reaching into
a bowl Lindy had left on the counter.

'I think I'll go and freshen up,' Lindy said.

'I'll come with you,' Hope responded, and Lindy
could see the speculation dancing in her sister's eyes.

'Don't push it now,' Lindy advised quietly as they
left the room. To her relief, Hope took the hint. She
knew she'd have to face the speculation and questions
sooner or later, but right now it was going to be hard
enough to justify her brazen behaviour to herself, let
alone anyone else!

CHAPTER TWO

LINDY didn't look up as her sister came in and lay on the patchwork counterpane of her bed. Hope lifted one long, tanned leg, revealed pleasingly in a pair of denim shorts, and examined her painted toenails silently.

'Good journey?' she said brightly.

Lindy knew this wasn't the question she was longing to ask. What she really wanted to know was how her restrained sister had managed to end up on Sam Rourke's lap in a passionate clinch after an extremely short acquaintance.

'I've no idea how it happened,' she said abruptly, glaring half-defiantly at Hope in the dressing-table mirror she was facing. She tapped ineffectually at her honey-blonde hair with a silver-backed brush and frowned at her reflection.

'The journey or...?' Hope raised her eyebrows dramatically.

'Or...' Lindy confirmed quickly, before her sister went into painful detail.

'Well, if you're going to go all spontaneous and passionate it might as well be with Sam. He is about as delicious as men get.' She ran her tongue across her lips as if relishing the thought and swung herself upright, tucking one leg neatly underneath the other in the lotus position.

'It wasn't what it looked like. I don't go for beef cake. People as obviously good-looking as him only exist in soaps—daytime soaps!'

'Miss hoity-toity!' Hope taunted. 'Let your mind wander back a few minutes.'

Lindy covered her face with her hands and groaned. 'Don't!' she pleaded, her bravado disintegrating. She spread her fingers and peeped out at her sister. 'I can't believe I...' She shrugged her shoulders and her hands fell away from her face. 'You know... It's awful!'

'Heavens, I'm supposed to be the tragedy queen of the family,' said Hope. 'Don't tell me he's got bad breath—I have some semi-lecherous scenes with the man.'

'I'm surprised you haven't been practising.' Lindy bit her lip when, after a startled silence, her sister burst out laughing. 'I'm glad *you* find this funny,' Lindy snapped, spinning around on her stool. The idea of her gorgeous sister sampling the pleasures of Sam's lips and heaven knew what else made her feel very bad-tempered. 'Is *he* still here?'

'Lloyd's gone but, if you mean Sam, he's staying here. I was going to surprise you.'

'Oh, you did, Hope, you did. I made a total fool of myself.'

'A few kisses!' Hope shrugged. 'It *was* just a few kisses, wasn't it? All right, don't blow a fuse,' she said hastily. 'Rigid principles are all well and good, but sometimes the best of us weaken given temptation.'

Lindy put aside her own problems for a moment as she recalled the insinuations Sam had made about Hope and the rather daunting man she had recently, if briefly, met. 'Are you speaking from personal experience here?'

'You and Sam did spend some time talking, then, before you ripped off his clothes.'

Lindy firmly put aside the startling image of Sam Rourke's perfect frame. She wasn't about to be diverted from her theme. The cautious expression she had seen briefly in her sister's eyes had been enough to worry her.

'I can't think of any reason to undress a man who is

capable of doing it for himself.' She couldn't let this
assumption pass unchallenged.

'I could enumerate them,' her sister offered gener-
ously.

'I think Sam didn't want me to be taken by surprise
by the gossip,' Lindy said swiftly—too swiftly. It was
faintly shocking to realise that her own brain was fertile
enough to make any lesson from Hope on the subject
redundant.

'Sam's no gossip,' Hope acceded. 'Unfortunately,
he's a minority of one. I'm not having an affair with
Lloyd.'

Lindy met her sister's eyes and gave a sigh of relief.
'I'm glad; I'd hate for you to be hurt. I know how...'
Her voice thickened.

Hope came over and gave her a quick hug. 'It was an
awfully long time ago,' she said softly, compassion in
her eyes. 'No matter how it looks, I'm not involved with
Lloyd, at least not in that way.'

'Do you think it's wise to spend the day with him and
fuel people's speculation?'

Hope got to her feet. 'People's nasty minds are not
my problem,' she observed sharply.

Lindy didn't think this was a very practical position
to take, but she didn't voice her doubts. 'Perhaps they'll
think you're having an affair with Sam—he is living
here.'

'He's only stopping for a couple more days. He has
a boat that he usually lives on. It's down here, but it's
in dry dock having its keel hauled or whatever they do
to boats. The hotels are overflowing with our lot and,
besides, the poor lamb likes his privacy. Anyway, he's
a much better cook than I am.'

'That's no great recommendation,' Lindy said, recalling some of her sister's more spectacular culinary ex-

ploits. 'Ducks have been known to sink when fed your soufflé.'

'I'll probably marry a chef,' Hope said thoughtfully. 'A tall one,' she added with a chuckle as she ducked her head to avoid a low beam. 'Do you like the room? Isn't the place a find?'

'It's lovely, Hope. Or am I supposed to call you Lacey here?'

'Don't you dare! Is it going to be a problem for you with Sam here?' she said, her expression growing serious. 'I could ask him to find somewhere else.'

'Don't be silly.' The last thing she wanted to do was play up the whole trivial incident. He was attractive and he'd kissed her—and she'd kissed him, a pedantic voice annoyingly added. She could share a roof with the man and show him how little she was affected by the experience. 'It was a momentary aberration, that's all.'

'If you say so.'

'I do,' Lindy responded firmly, not much caring for the tone of her sister's voice.

It turned out that Hope hadn't exaggerated the dratted man's culinary talents. She and Hope returned from a stroll along the beach later that evening to find the table set and delicious smells emanating from the galley kitchen.

'That smell's terrific, you lovely man, you.' Hope peeled off the jacket she had worn against the evening chill, shook out her golden mane and threw her arms around Sam's neck. She ritually kissed him on both cheeks and Lindy, watching, couldn't believe that any man wouldn't be bowled over by her warmth and vitality. 'I might just keep you on.'

'Sorry, honey, but my heart belongs to Jennifer.'

'What a waste,' she replied with a grin.

Lindy quietly took her place at the table and hoped

her strong desire to ask about the identity of Jennifer was not as easy to detect as she suspected it was. Did Jennifer know he went around kissing perfect strangers?

'Do you feel better after your rest, Rosalind?' Sam asked as Hope helped herself to a generous portion of home-made pasta.

'Much, thank you.' Like a coward, she'd avoided contact with him earlier in the evening by pleading exhaustion—a cop-out, and he probably knew it. It had worked, though. She could now be perfectly objective about his smouldering sexuality.

She heaved a sigh. Who am I kidding? she thought. Seeing him now made her realise that pretending the incident earlier hadn't happened just wasn't feasible. It went against the grain, but she'd have to accept that for some inexplicable reason, and even though he symbolised the things she despised in men—the excessive good looks, the calculating charm—she was attracted to him in a basic sort of way. I'm damned if I'm going to act like some star-struck teenager, she decided, lifting her head and looking him firmly in the eye. Both eyes, actually—deep, mesmerising eyes.

She broke a bread roll and found her hands were trembling. 'Hope tells me you have a boat.'

'She's having her hull shot-blasted, but she'll be back on the water by the weekend. So you'll be rid of me. That is what you want, isn't it?' The latter was said in a voice meant only for her ears, and Lindy sensed the confusion she was fighting was mirrored in her eyes.

'You'll have to get used to eating out, Lindy, or cook,' Hope said with her mouth full. Her sister did everything with such enthusiasm and lack of inhibition that Lindy suddenly felt stilted and awkward by comparison. She was sure Sam must see the contrast. Why on earth should I care if he does? she wondered, angry at this bizarre preoccupation she had with the man.

'You'll have to come for a sail on *Jennifer* when the schedule permits.' He caught Lindy's flicker of comprehension. 'You thought she was a woman, my *Jennifer*?' He filled her glass with wine and leaned back in his chair. The candlelight shadowed the planes and hollows of his aesthetically sculpted face and left his eyes areas of mystery.

'Named for a woman, it's almost the same thing,' she responded, realising how astute he was at interpreting the slightest nuance in body language.

'Not one of mine. I never bothered changing the name when I got her ten years back. The longest relationship I've ever had with a female,' he acknowledged with a lecherous grin.

Hope gave a laugh, accepting the gauntlet. 'Hark at the sex symbol of our times,' she teased. '"Not one of mine."'

Rather to Lindy's surprise, Sam seemed to appreciate Hope's mockery. 'Keeping the name means I don't have to worry about changing the paintwork every time I part company with a lady.'

'This boy isn't as stupid as he looks,' Hope said, impressed. 'I'll get it,' she added as the phone shrilled.

'How's the nose?' Lindy asked, quelling the panic that threatened as Hope disappeared.

'Lloyd thinks it'll be fine if we stick to my left profile.'

'Seriously?' she said, examining his perfect right profile.

'Candlelight conceals all sorts of nasty things,' he said, running his palm lightly over the candle in the middle of the table.

'You shouldn't play with fire,' she warned sharply. She wanted to snatch his hand away from the flame, but she knew that touching Sam Rourke wasn't a good idea.

He'd awoken feelings inside her she'd thought had died for ever.

'Life would be boring.' His deep tone had never been more honeyed.

Lindy found she couldn't pull her eyes away from his deceptively sleepy gaze. Heavy, sexy eyelids drooped over the steady glitter of his azure stare.

'I like boring,' she said firmly. Boring, safe and familiar—and Sam was none of those things.

'Shame.'

'I'll have to love you and leave you.'

Lindy tore her stare from Sam to look with incomprehension at her sister, who had entered the room carrying an overnight bag over her shoulder. 'Leave... where?'

'I'll explain later. Sam will show you where to go tomorrow.'

'You're not coming back tonight?' I must have misunderstood, she thought in bewilderment.

'Can't stop, I'm in a hurry.' Hope avoided her sister's eyes.

Lindy sat in shock, listening a few moments later to the sound of a car engine being started. The sound disappeared and she expelled the breath she'd been holding.

'This is bizarre,' she said, half to herself. It was so unlike Hope to do something so inconsiderate. Leave her alone with— Her heart gave a triple beat as she shrank from this new situation. Slowly she turned to look at Sam.

'I've been here the best part of a week and Hope's only spent two nights at home.' He gave the information slowly, his eyes gauging her reaction.

'Meaning?' Lindy said, with a dangerous inflection in her voice.

'She's your sister.'

'She's not having an affair.' She was stubbornly defiant and confident that, whatever her sister was up to, it wasn't that.

'You asked her?'

'I did.'

'Fair enough, but I have to say she seems to be doing her best to disprove that statement.'

'Hope wouldn't run just because some man picks up the phone. That would be pathetic,' she observed with distaste. 'There has to be some other explanation,' she reasoned.

'That could be love,' Sam suggested lightly. 'Wouldn't you do the same for the man you loved?'

'In a pig's eye!'

'I believe you,' he said thoughtfully, examining her flushed cheeks and indignant expression. 'I take it you did a lot of running for someone unworthy of the exercise?'

'When I was young and extremely foolish,' she admitted stiffly. Inwardly, she was appalled that this man could see so much behind her unguarded words. What was she doing being unguarded? Hadn't her defences been built to survive any assault? 'I'd bore you with the salacious details but I've forgotten them.'

'I doubt that— Don't,' he said, catching her wrist as she pushed back her chair to get up.

Lindy looked at the brown hand covering her narrow wrist and his fingers slowly unfurled. She could still feel the impression of his hand, like a brand on her skin. Shakily, her anger suddenly dispersing like hot air from a pricked balloon, she sat down.

'I know my sister.' Her eyes met his surprisingly compassionate ones.

'There's no point us arguing about it, is there?' he said persuasively. 'I like Hope, I like Lloyd. I've no axe to grind. Just remember family loyalties can take a back seat when passion gets involved.'

The warning was well meant, she could see that. She thought of Anna, married now to Adam, and knew he was right. Priorities did change. A year ago she would have told Anna about her problems at work, but now she hadn't. 'I wouldn't like to see Hope get hurt.'

'She's a big girl and well able to take care of herself. All you can do is be there if she falls flat on her face.'

'You could be right,' she mused with a sigh.

'Nine times out of ten.'

'Don't you take *anything* seriously?' Part of her wanted to respond to the beguiling smile in his eyes. This weakness made her angry.

'I think that's a virtue,' he declared. 'You think it's a fault,' he added sadly. 'Actually, I take my work seriously, although I try hard not to let it take over my life. That's why you can relax about me...us. I've worked hard to get myself prepared for this role. I can't even blame the director if I blow it—as he's me! A bit like a fighter before a big fight, I'm saving myself.'

She could see the glimmer of sincerity behind his laid-back humour. This opportunity was obviously as important to him as Hope's was to her.

'You really are an egomaniac.' He must consider me a total pushover—with good cause, she thought grimly.

'Turn off the act, Rosalind. I think I'll call you Rosalind—it's a lovely name and it suits you.'

'You're the actor.'

'I recognise talent when I see it, Rosalind. You're so damned good, I believed in the cool, emotionless, tepid image that you've got off pat. You blew it pretty thoroughly, though. But don't panic, I won't tell the world that you're passionate and—'

'Sheer male fantasy!' she interrupted, her voice a high-pitched squeak rather than the sneer it was meant to be.

'Don't remind me of fantasies, Rosalind, or I might just let you distract me, despite my schedule.'

'Where in the schedule does sex come?' she asked, irrationally piqued that he could apparently cope a lot better than she could with the spectre of lust. 'Between therapy and your personal trainer?'

'I find talking to friends just as effective and much cheaper than a therapist, and I know my body better than a stranger—we've been together thirty-one years. Success hasn't meant I have to conform to a set standard of behaviour for Hollywood actors. It's meant I have the freedom to do things my way.'

'Then why, Mr Golden Box Office, have you got your knickers in a twist over this film? Or do you always take a vow of celibacy when you're working?'

'Firstly, I didn't mean to imply I'd taken a vow of celibacy. I think a relationship with you might prove pretty distracting. Correct me if I'm wrong, but I'd assumed you didn't go in for one-night stands, or even steamy weekends?' One dark brow quirked upwards towards his hairline and she flushed rosily.

'I don't!'

'Neither, despite what you might read in the more lurid periodicals, do I. Although for you I might have been willing to compromise.

'This film matters to me, Rosalind,' he said more earnestly. 'I'm typecast. I'm not griping about that; the business has been good to me. But I want a broader canvas. I'd every intention of financing this myself until Lloyd stepped in. He's willing to take a risk on me— and it is a risk; make no mistake about that. As far as Joe Public's concerned, I'm Sam Rourke playing Sam Rourke and everyone loves me. If I play not just a very unlovable character but one without a single redeeming feature, there's a strong possibility they might not like it, even if I don't fall flat on my face. When you're at

the top people are always waiting for you to fall. I've
no intention of doing that.'

'I can understand ambition and dedication,' she said
faintly. His open way of speaking was pretty shattering.
Of course, this painful honesty could be part of a more
devious ploy, but she didn't think so.

He nodded. 'This is the right time.' Whatever doubts
or fears he might have, he sounded superbly confident
that he was up to the challenge. 'But not for us...'

'I wish you wouldn't say things like that,' she
pleaded. The idea that Sam Rourke found her attractive
was too much to cope with.

'I think anything between us would be complicated,
fraught with big emotional drama and angst.'

She had the best skin he'd ever seen, creamy pale with
a sort of translucent quality, and eyes that could be
stormily passionate one moment and cool and serene the
next.

Sam's observation had the effect of robbing Lindy
momentarily of breath. 'How fortunate you've decided
to save us both from all that. I mean, I would naturally
have been too weak to resist your fatal charm.' He was
the oddest mixture of self-deprecation and confidence
she'd ever come across.

'Ego the size of the prairie, that's me,' he agreed with
a grin. 'It must have been something pretty heavy to
make a serious-minded lady like yourself step off the
promotion treadmill,' he said curiously. The action
didn't seem in keeping with the woman he'd met.

The sly turn of subject had her reeling off balance.
'It's only temporary. My boss made it clear that if I
wasn't prepared to sleep with him I could forget about
extending my contract... I don't know why I told you
that,' she said, expressing her amazement out loud. 'I've
only told Hope about the sordid details. I didn't even
tell Anna.'

'Your other sister? Why not?' He hadn't visibly reacted to her admission at all and she felt extremely embarrassed about voicing it.

'She's married now, to Adam, who used to be my
boss. If she'd told Adam he'd have been as mad as hell,
and most likely he'd have done something about it.' She
gave a frown of irritation as Sam's somewhat grim expression showed approval. 'It was my problem and I
didn't want to be bailed out.' She gave a dry laugh. 'I
could have asked Anna not to tell Adam, but no matter
what she decides to keep secret from him the second he
walks into a room she blurts everything out. It's a sort
of Pavlovian response.' Lindy gave a smile of rueful
affection.

'Anna wouldn't have approved of me resigning any
more than Hope did. She'd have made an official com-
plaint, no matter what the consequences to herself. As
for Hope—' she gave a small wry laugh '—she'd have
delivered one of her famous left hooks. Me, what do I
do? I run away, that's what I do.' She felt a surge of
self-disgust.

Lindy raised her paper napkin to her face to blot the
rush of weak tears that suddenly spilled down her
cheeks. 'God, I'm so pathetic!' she wailed. With a fierce
sniff and a gulp she stemmed the flow before it became
an avalanche. 'Don't say anything sympathetic!' she ordered gruffly. 'Or I'll start all over again.' She hardly
dared look at him to see what he made of her gratuitous
confession. She certainly didn't want him to think that
she was angling for sympathy.

'I wasn't going to.'

'You weren't?' Indignation shone through the tears in
her eyes and she rubbed her nose furiously with bits of
a tissue she'd shredded. It fell like confetti onto the table.

'Wouldn't that be pointless? You'd reject any advice
or sympathy I gave you out of hand. You're not even

prepared to admit you're emotionally vulnerable, so you can't accept sympathy. You run away from situations that are out of your control, but then I'm sure you're aware of that.'

'What would you know?' she snarled.

'A mere man,' he murmured, with a maliciously innocent smile. 'The enemy? I'd say your self-esteem, or rather lack of it, is the enemy here.'

'I suppose you'd think I was healthier if I had a love affair with myself, like you!'

'I'm aware of my faults, but I don't crucify myself over them. Be a little gentler with yourself, Rosalind.'

'I thought you weren't going to offer me any advice.'

'And here I was thinking I was being subtle.' He gave a sigh. 'You're too sharp for me, Rosalind.'

'Will you stop calling me that?' she said from between gritted teeth.

'No,' he replied, with a sunny good humour which she found quite impossible to combat or dent. 'We might have decided to put lust off the agenda,' he said with another sigh, 'but I'm damned if I'm going to shorten such a lovely name.'

'We?' she said witheringly. 'We! I seem to recall that being a unilateral decision.' She went bright pink under the gleam kindled in the depths of his eyes. 'Not that I have any problem with that,' she added hastily. 'But you were debating a purely fictitious scenario.'

'Don't underestimate how frustrating I'm finding this situation, Rosalind,' Sam warned. 'Or I might be tempted to make you eat those words.'

'Oh, pooh! What role did you take that line from?' she asked contemptuously. Let him shove that in his brash, egotistical pipe and choke on it!

'You little...' The handsome, smiling face dropped its guard for a moment, revealing an inner strength of feeling—of passionate intensity—that took her breath away.

He turned in his seat at the head of the table until their knees clashed. Smoothing his thumbs along the curve of her angular jawbone, he took her face in his hands.

'I don't need cue-cards to cope with real life,' he grated, looking not at all like the easygoing, humorous man he'd been moments before. 'Are you afraid of me, Rosalind?' His smile left his eyes cold and she shivered.

'No,' she breathed defiantly.

'Maybe I've been lulling you into a false sense of security before I move in for the kill?' His eyes were hypnotic and his sonorous tone intimidating.

She shook her head, the movement restricted by the grip of his long fingers.

'Let's hope I scare the cinema audiences more than I do you,' he said, releasing her abruptly. A mocking smile spread over his face as he took in her expression of shock.

'You...you were trying to...' She wanted to take a swing at him and wipe away that smug, supercilious smirk. He'd been trying to scare her and he'd actually slipped into character. Of all the shallow, superficial monsters, he had to take the cake!

'It was all wasted on you. You were totally unimpressed by my psychopathic aura of sinister threat, weren't you?'

'I was scared to death, you calculating beast, and you know it!' she responded furiously. It was the fact that she hadn't just been scared by his transformation, she'd been fascinated by it that worried her most.

'Calculating?' he said with an odd, strained expression. 'I was just using what comes naturally to get me—us—out of a potentially explosive situation. I found myself with your face here.' He carefully repositioned his fingers around her jaw, identifying the exact position from memory. 'I knew exactly what I was going to do next, and at the last second I stopped myself by going into a diversionary routine. It's amazing how women go for those mean, moody types who use them,' he observed with a sour smile.

'What's that supposed to mean?' she asked warily.

'I could see it in your face,' he replied. 'You were totally enthralled by Jack.'

'Jack?'

'Your friendly neighbourhood psychopath, Jack Callender, the character I'm playing.'

The name clicked with Lindy as she recalled the plot of one of her favourite thrillers. When Hope had told her she was starring in the film version of *The Legacy*, Lindy had originally assumed that Sam Rourke would be playing the nice hero, the only one capable of seeing that Dr Jack Callender was a nasty piece of work who killed off folk who got in the way of his plans.

Hope was playing the part of Jack Callender's long-lost stepsister, who appeared to claim her share of their mother's estate. After her private preview Lindy could more readily accept Sam's casting against type.

If Sam could re-create the claustrophobic atmosphere of menace the author had created in the book, they'd be onto a winner. Having spent nearly three hundred pages praying for the heroine to escape from his homicidal clutches, Lindy, like all other readers, had been stunned when the heroine had turned out not to be the innocent victim, but a fake who wasn't squeamish when it came to murder. The twist in the tale had been cunningly clever. It was certainly a meaty role for Hope.

'If you're implying I'm some sort of masochist who's attracted by manipulative brutes, you couldn't be more wrong,' Lindy protested hotly.

'Not consciously,' he conceded, stroking a thumb down her cheek. 'But women have this thing about danger.'

'I think it's you who has the problem,' she returned

tartly. 'At least I don't go around pretending to be someone I'm not.'

'I have no personality crisis, Rosalind, but I think there's a little bit of Jack's dark side in us all,' Sam said slowly. 'I think you were a lot safer with him than me right now.'

'Why?' She hardly recognised her own voice. The expression on his face, a raw frustration, filled her with more fascination than his earlier performance had. Yet there was danger here too—danger in asking the question, danger in prolonging this situation. 'What were you going to do that was so bad? Or don't you have a personality of your own?'

He sucked in his breath and his chest rose. 'You want to know what I was going to do?' One hand slid to her shoulderblade and the other moved to the back of her head. 'This.'

Whatever devil had possessed her to push him to this point she couldn't imagine. She hadn't known such a creature dwelt within her, but then she hadn't known a kiss like this existed either. It set out to dominate and subdue and it did both, but more—much more.

There was no preliminary, just fierce, hard possession. His tongue sank into the warm, moist recess of her mouth hungrily. The whimper in her throat, the fine tremor that rippled through his powerful body were all elements of the total mind-numbing confusion.

'Satisfied?' he grated, his hand automatically going to loosen a non-existent tie at his throat. Discovering the open neck of his shirt, he scowled and muttered under his breath. He was genuinely shocked at his brief loss of control, and alarmed that this woman whom he scarcely knew had been the catalyst.

'I asked for that,' she said in a stunned voice.

'Not a very politically correct statement, but you'll get no arguments from me on that score,' he said in a tone that showed clearly that the brief embrace, if such a wild, elemental thing could be so classified, had not improved his humour.

Like molten lava solidifying, her body was regaining its normal control. Her skin was tacky with sweat from the enormous burst of temperature, but her face had gone deathly pale.

'Dear God,' he said, looking at her stricken face. 'That was unforgivable.' He raked his fingers through his thatch of thick, jet-dark hair and looked abstracted.

'It was only a kiss,' she said absently.

He touched the corner of her mouth where the delicate membrane had broken and a faint smear of blood tinged her pale lips.

'You chose the wrong time to start playing with fire,' he said gently. 'Go away, Rosalind, before I try to kiss you better.'

The ambiguity of her response shone briefly in her eyes, before she did exactly what he suggested and fled to her room.

CHAPTER THREE

LINDY stared at the sheaf of papers Sam pushed into her hands.

'This is nonsense,' she said slowly as she deciphered the printed gobbledygook. At first glance the characters' names were the only things that made any sense to her.

'So is medical jargon to me and the scriptwriter. Fill in the blanks with authentic terminology and Ned will make any adjustments. Is there something you don't understand?'

Lindy compressed her lips and bit back a vitriolic retort. He had said she'd be working hard for her money, and he wasn't wrong! She was used to unsociable hours, but she hadn't expected to see the sun rise over the ocean on her way to work this morning.

A peremptory banging on her bedroom door had woken her at an ungodly hour. Sam had proceeded to inform her through an inch of wood that she had half an hour before he was off. This was the reason why she didn't have a scrap of make-up on and her hair, which needed shampooing, was scraped back in a ponytail. She felt cross, tired, nervous and very ill-used. Where were sisters when you needed them? she wondered.

Sam Rourke was the most inconsiderate man she'd ever come across. To add insult to injury, he had scarcely appeared to notice her on the journey to the Gothic-looking mansion at which, it transpired, they were filming. A lot had been going on behind those spectacular eyes, but none of it involved her! That suited her just fine, she told herself. She had watched as Sam's presence on the set had a similar effect to a bracing

44

wind, and those who, like herself, felt sluggish were
soon infected by the man's vitality and enthusiasm.

'Fine,' he said, taking her silence as acquiescence.
'I'll look it over later.' Lindy watched him stride away
with a purposeful air and wished she knew what she was
doing.

'You look lost.'

Lindy turned to the owner of the sympathetic voice.
'I'm moving in that direction,' she admitted.

'I'm Ned Stewart, the writer.'

Lindy smiled. He was being modest adding his job
description. Like millions of others she was a fan of
N.A. Stewart's best-selling psychological thrillers. This
was the first time that anyone had attempted to transfer
his work to the big screen and Lindy, who had loved the
book, would have hoped that the production would do
it justice even if she hadn't had a personal interest in the
enterprise.

'Lindy Lacey,' she said, smiling warmly. With brown
eyes, brown hair and a slow smile, he didn't look like
someone who could produce such dark menace on the
printed page; he looked much too wholesome.

'You shouldn't worry about admitting you need help
from Sam, Lindy Lacey. He's very good at making
tough concepts simple, and he's no tyrant.' He gave her
a shrewd grin. 'You're a latecomer; it's bound to take
you a while to settle in. I've outlined the scene and
what's happening, who's talking and for approximately
how long. You just need to substitute suitable medical
lingo. If you need a hand, just yell.'

Lindy didn't yell. Several hours later she was curled
up in a corner of Hope's trailer, eating a plate of food
and feeling cautiously pleased with the results of her
efforts, when her sister came in. She didn't notice Lindy
at first. She sat down in front of the mirror and closed
her eyes.

'You look exhausted,' Lindy said.

Hope started. 'You've finally perfected the art of invisibility, I see.' Her smile flashed out and the lines of strain around her eyes vanished.

'Perhaps you should have earlier nights.'

'There's no need for painful subtlety, Lindy,' Hope said wearily. 'I'm not about to do anything to jeopardise this movie,' she added firmly. 'I want to be taken seriously as an actress, not someone who got the job because of her famous face and long legs. I'm on time and I don't do tantrums.'

'How did you get the job?'

'You mean did I sleep with the producer? Or would it bother you more if it was the director?'

Anger flashed in her sister's eyes, but Lindy didn't back down; she stared calmly back. Something was clearly bothering Hope, who normally had a sunny disposition.

'I meant, how did you get the job?'

'If you must know, I did a test for a part in *Shadow of Her Smile*,' Hope said more coolly, referring to the previous year's summer box-office hit which Lloyd Elliot had produced and directed. 'I didn't get it, but Lloyd remembered me, and when he got involved in the project with Sam he mentioned my name. I did a test that blew Sam's mind,' she said with engaging frankness. 'Before you say it, yes, I am grateful to Lloyd but not *that* grateful.'

'Something's going on.'

'Just forget it, Lindy, forget it,' Hope pleaded wearily.

Lindy sighed. What choice did she have? she thought, giving a philosophical shrug. 'Is the food always this good?' She pushed aside the empty plate before she got to her feet. The catering trailer appeared to produce vast quantities of food all day. 'I'll be the size of a house if I go on like this.'

'Not with your metabolic rate,' Hope scoffed. 'It's my hips that doughnuts love.' She gave a sigh before placing her hands on said luscious curves. 'Incidentally, I think Sam has sent out the cavalry to find you.'

'I wasn't hiding,' Lindy observed. Wasn't there going to be a second of her day when the darned man wasn't brought into the conversation?

'Are you quite sure about that?' Hope gave a little smile which set Lindy's teeth on edge. 'I hope you and Sam didn't miss me too much...?'

Lindy kept her face placid. 'I can't speak for him but, quite frankly, I did. I could have done with some hand-holding to break the ice.'

The spikiness evaporated instantly from her sister's lovely face. 'Of course you did,' she said with contrition. 'I know I've left you to sink or swim, but I can't imagine you drowning.'

For some reason the colour of Sam Rourke's eyes popped into Lindy's head. She flicked her ponytail with her fingers and banished the recollection of vivid blue. The most a girl could hope for would be to tread water when she looked into those sinful orbs.

'It's mostly high-tension monotony really,' Hope soothed. 'There's no reason to feel intimidated. Sam's pretty demanding, but he doesn't stamp around ranting—he's much too subtle for that,' she reflected drily. 'I suspect he'll employ whatever tactics he sees fit to drag what he wants out of us. He obviously has a clear mental image of how things should be done, but he's quite willing to listen to ideas, up to a point. He's incredibly devious.' She sounded quite admiring about that.

'The crew seem to be high-spirited,' Lindy said. If the couple of hours she'd spent watching that morning were anything to go by, that was an understatement.

'The humour can get pretty vicious at times, not to

mention X-rated,' Hope agreed. 'And, no matter what everyone thinks, I wouldn't be surprised if I'm the only one *not* having a fling. If a fraction of what's going on behind the cameras was to end up on film the censors would blow a fuse! So don't say I didn't warn you!'

'Does "everyone" include Sam?' She couldn't match Hope's acting ability and the question didn't quite achieve casualness. The knowing look her sister cast her made Lindy want to moan. For someone who wanted to emphasise she wasn't interested, that had been a foolish thing to say.

'It rather depends on who you listen to,' Hope responded slowly. 'Magda, the one in Make-Up—but then you wouldn't know her, would you?' she said, her eyes skimming her sister's pale features.

Lindy's hand went self-consciously to her scraped-back hair. 'I'll leave the glamour to you.'

'Magda in Make-Up, tall, blonde...'

'Who isn't here?' Lindy felt an instant, deep antipathy to this unknown female.

'Touchy, aren't we?' Hope's curving dark eyebrows shot upwards. 'As I was saying, she is sort of dropping strong hints that the thing she had once with Sam has risen phoenix-like from the ashes. Personally, I think it's wishful thinking, but you never know... I think he's like me—he has something to prove and not much energy left over to play.'

'Perhaps that's what he wants everyone to think,' Lindy observed sourly.

Hope regarded her sister thoughtfully for a moment, a frown creasing her brow. 'Sam seems to have got under your skin—which is nothing to do with me,' she added hastily. 'But you do realise that you're going to be working mostly with him? I mean, he is the doctor of the piece and we're about to shoot the medical scenes.

You're literally going to be walking him through those shots.'

'I'll cope,' Lindy replied with a confidence she was far from feeling.

In the event, anticipation turned out to be a lot more gruelling than the real thing. Sam was a quick learner and his astute questions and eye for detail made her task a lot easier. Watching him deal with a fictional medical emergency, she found herself wishing she had looked half as confident when she had first donned a white coat.

At the end of her first day Lindy felt exhausted, but fairly satisfied that she hadn't completely messed up. Her sister emerged from her trailer, having discarded the long, floaty floral dresses her character favoured for knee-length khaki shorts, a cropped tee shirt and boots that had a few miles on the clock. A fashion disaster, but Hope could have made bin-liners the height of fashion, should she have felt the inclination, Lindy reflected a shade wistfully. To Lindy's amusement, Hope appeared oblivious to the covertly lustful looks that she drew as they walked together to Hope's car.

After a couple of minutes of deep abstraction Hope gave a sudden exclamation. 'I'm sorry,' she said, emerging from the distracted trance. 'I haven't asked you how it went. It's really difficult to throw off the part. The character sort of gets under your skin,' she admitted ruefully. 'Everything's so slow, it's hard sometimes to maintain a level of concentration, and just as hard to let go once you've worked yourself into it.'

'I understand—or at least I think I do,' Lindy said in the interests of accuracy. 'It wasn't as bad as I'd imagined.' She stopped as they reached Hope's car. To her dismay, Lloyd Elliot was leaning against the bonnet, in deep conversation with Sam.

The mention of distribution runs and press releases

meant little to Lindy, but she did notice that when Sam disagreed on some point the other man listened and eventually nodded. Lloyd Elliot was one of the most important men in the industry and he obviously respected Sam Rourke. Lindy found she wasn't surprised. Her own opinion that Sam was a shallow piece of beef cake had already been seriously eroded.

'Hope.' Lloyd Elliot cut short his conversation as he caught sight of her sister. 'I was hoping we could get together tonight?' There was more apology than lover-like promise in his voice.

Hope gave a deep sigh. 'Tonight? I've not spent any time with Lindy yet.' She regarded him reproachfully.

'I wouldn't ask if...'

Hope pressed her fingertips together and raised them to her lips. 'OK,' she said tightly. 'Sorry, Lindy.' She summoned a tight smile for her sister. 'Take my car.' She handed Lindy the keys from her pocket.

Lindy shrugged her shoulders. 'I'll be fine,' she said. The more she tried to figure out the relationship between her sister and this man, the more mystified she became.

'See you later,' Hope said, linking her arm through Lloyd's as a group of technicians went past. It was almost as if, Lindy thought, her bewilderment deepening, she *wanted* them to think that she and Lloyd were an item. It made no sense.

She shook her head in frustration and sensed Sam's silent regard. 'Do you know what's going on?' she demanded.

'Leave me out of this,' he said, holding up his hands. 'Hold up a minute, Will!' He waved towards the burly figure of Will Gibson, the director of photography. Lindy had already been introduced to the multi-Oscar-winning technician. 'We need to discuss that helicopter shot of Hope on the rocks tomorrow. You've met Rosalind?'

'Met her! I've fallen passionately in love with the

lady.' Will Gibson worked hard to maintain his hell-raising image, but Lindy thought that underneath he was probably rather nice.

'I meet his two criteria of desirability,' Lindy said calmly. Both men were looking at her. 'I've a pulse and I'm female. So I've tried not to be too overcome by the honour.'

'Old son,' Will said, with a delighted chuckle, 'this one's not stupid.'

Sam shot her a glance, his eyes meshing with hers for a long, silent moment. 'I'd noticed,' he drawled. 'Can you find your way back?' he said doubtfully. 'I'll be tied up here for another couple of hours.'

It was the first time all day he'd looked at her in a less than impersonal manner and, to her dismay, Lindy felt her body react forcibly to the fact.

'I've an excellent sense of direction,' she assured him crisply. At least her voice wasn't fluttering as feebly as her pulse rate. Years of practice at sounding cool and in control in the midst of confusion stood her in good stead.

Sam raised one eyebrow sceptically, but didn't make an issue of the matter as she climbed into Hope's car.

'I take it you've put in your order for a rough sea tomorrow?' Will said. 'Are you with us?' he asked as his director's attention remained focused on the dust cloud thrown up by the retreating vehicle's wheels.

Sam turned his head and gave the older man a grim glare that cut short any further shrewd and probably lewd comments Will had been about to make.

'The meteorological guys are promising us a low tomorrow and some hefty winds,' he replied. 'Not bad enough to keep the helicopter grounded, but enough to give us a bleak, stormy backdrop. The sea should look like a black devil's cauldron. I want the shot to cut from Hope to me disposing of the body, and end with Hope just an indistinguishable speck on the rock. There's no escape, danger on all sides. I want everyone to feel her isolation.'

Will's beady eyes took on a gleam of professional interest, but Sam didn't notice.

'She's doomed,' he intoned.

'You've got it in one.' Sam felt an intense surge of irritation that Rosalind kept disrupting his flow of thoughts. Why did she keep intruding? He was beginning to suspect that treating her impersonally all day hadn't really achieved his purpose. In fact, his self-imposed restraint had only managed to draw attention to her. He had given her a hard ride today and she'd risen to the challenge damned well, he decided with admiration.

He gave himself a mental shake and concentrated on what Will was saying. On the whole, the elements were a lot more predictable than his own emotions just now!

The sunken Jacuzzi could have happily housed a soccer team. Alone, Lindy lay back and studied the seascape spread before her. She'd opened the sliding doors to let the distant sound of the waves into the room. Closing her eyes, she concentrated on the soothing murmur and let the tension ease its way from her spine.

She tried to banish all thoughts of Sam from her mind, but this was difficult to achieve. Impossible to achieve, to be totally accurate. She had to settle for cursing the fates that had brought her into his orbit. The hot water was bliss, though, and she lazily rubbed with her toes the area on her calf where she'd been bitten by mosquitoes. Extending her leg from the water, she regarded the reddened area with a frown.

'You could do with something on those. There's some antihistamine cream in the bathroom.'

Lindy let out a startled shriek. 'How long have you been there?' she asked, after she'd thrashed about inelegantly in the water in a most undignified manner. 'How dare you sneak up on me?' she continued accusingly.

Sam, who was sprawled in a deep rattan chair piled high with ethnic printed cushions, just raised one brow, a very eloquent brow. 'I didn't want to disturb you,' he said quietly. His deep blue eyes were gazing with disturbing intensity at her face.

Lindy felt odd, trembling sensations sliding through her body and she gave a short laugh. He was aiming for the impossible. Somehow she had to come to terms with the fact that this man would always disturb her!

'Didn't anyone warn you to use insect repellent?'

'I didn't think they'd get to unexposed bits.'

'Very persistent little brutes. If you have any trouble reaching the parts—no, maybe that wouldn't be such a good idea,' he finished, giving a wry grin.

Lindy listened to his deep, attractive voice and suddenly wondered what she'd say if he suggested sharing the tub. The thought of his big muscular body, slick with water and within almost obligatory touching distance, made her go hot. Her chest felt tight, as if she couldn't breathe, and the tension in the room almost crackled with high-voltage tension.

'That wouldn't be such a good idea either.' His dry-as-dust tone sliced through the atmosphere.

Her eyelids, which had been drooping over narrowed eyes, suddenly opened wide, and she let out a cry as she bit the tip of her tongue which had been tracing the outline of her dry lips. Was I really doing anything so blatant? she wondered with horror. She could taste the tang of blood on her tongue. He couldn't possibly know what she'd been thinking! Could he? Mortification blasted her.

'I was thinking the same thing,' he said, by way of explanation. Or was it to soften her humiliation?

'I don't know how you can carry on a conversation

when I'm not saying anything.' An extra-fresh gust of wind made her shiver and lower her shoulders beneath the water.

Sam got up and closed the deck door. 'Body language can be pretty eloquent,' he said, looking down at her from his superior vantage point. 'Do you want a drink?' he asked abruptly, removing his gaze from her. 'Beer, wine...?'

'I'll have a beer if there's one going,' she replied. Her face was burning as she imagined just what her body had been saying.

His absence gave her the opportunity to get out of the tub. She swathed herself in an ankle-length towelling robe. To think she'd actually toyed with the idea of taking a dip nude! Considering how vulnerable she'd felt in the black one-piece swimsuit she'd elected to wear, it didn't bear thinking about. She was tying the belt very firmly around her waist when Sam returned, carrying two glasses.

'False security, Rosalind,' he murmured, placing the glasses on a ceramic-topped table. He reached towards her and gave the cord a sharp tug. The robe fell open and she gave a startled gasp. 'It's easy to see you were never a Boy Scout,' he chided as his fingers deftly re-knotted the tie firmly about her middle. Fingers looped in the belt, he gave a gentle jerk that brought her closer to him. 'Aren't you going to say thank you?'

She slowly raised her eyes to his face. The frightening sensation of losing control of the situation deepened as she absorbed the harsh tension in his expression and the searing heat that glittered in his eyes.

'You're very good...at kn-knots.' It was a distinct possibility that, if he let go, she'd just fold up and collapse in a heap at his feet. I'm feeble, she told herself—feeble-minded and pathetic!

'I do a lot of messing around in boats. It's a skill that

comes in handy. Did you know you talk to yourself?'
The sudden sharp query made her blink.

'What?'

'When I came in you were talking to yourself.'

Alarm gave her knees the strength to take her weight.
Her chin took on a defensive angle and she pulled as far
away from him as his thumbs, hooked in the fabric of
her belt, would permit.

'I was not!'

'Nothing very intelligible, and it was interspersed with
a lot of sighing. Does "Stupid, stupid, stupid" sound at
all familiar?' He watched the tell-tale colour wash over
her skin and his lips curved in a taunting smile. 'After
"Damn and blast him to hell!" you stayed under water
so long I was about to leap in and pull you out.'

'How dare you spy on me? You're nothing but a disgusting peeping Tom.' She'd been so absorbed by her
own thoughts that not only had she not been aware she
hadn't been alone, she hadn't known she'd voiced her
thoughts out loud.

'Tell me, Rosalind, was I wrong to take your curses
personally?'

Throat dry and her body racked with weak longing,
she shook her head defiantly.

'Well, if it's any comfort, I feel as if I'm exactly
where you verbally confined me. To be frank...'

'I'm not sure I can take frank,' she admitted quickly.
Why on earth couldn't this man avoid delicate subjects
and fudge the issue like anyone normal? It was her own
response to the whole question of sex being reopened
that she wanted to avoid. Painful though this frustration
was, she at least had her self-respect and pride. That was
very important to Lindy; she'd lost both once and had
vowed never to be in that situation again.

'I'm not sure I can take much more of this situation,'
he said abruptly. The raw quality that throbbed in his

deep voice made her fingers curl into tight fists. 'I don't know what it is about you.' He frowned deeply as he examined her upturned features, as if fascinated by the pale purity of her delicate bone structure. She saw the muscles in his brown neck ripple as he swallowed hard.

'As I'm not your type...'

'I don't have a type,' he said impatiently.

'You said...' she persisted huffily.

'I talk garbage.'

She was going to remember he'd said that, but right now the urgency in his voice was holding her complete attention.

'Will you just listen for a second? Sexual attraction isn't something you can analyse, but whatever the formula is—we have it,' he said bluntly.

'You take an awful lot for granted.' It would have been much easier to sound scathing if she could have believed this was all an act, one he'd used before, but there was nothing polished about his delivery. It looked suspiciously as if he really was finding the situation as hard as she was.

'I'm expending a hell of a lot of energy keeping you at arm's length. I don't think it's one of my better ideas. I think my original plan is counter-productive.'

'Refresh my memory. Is this the one where we don't have sex?'

'Not one of my more realistic ideas.'

Lindy gaped at him. He really was unbelievably arrogant. 'It worked for me.'

He regarded her with an amused expression of affection in his hot, midsummer-blue eyes. 'Are you trying to tell me you don't find me attractive?'

'It must be your modesty that turned my head.' There was soul-stealing devilment in his eyes and she sensed her struggle to resist was doomed.

'Cut it out, Rosalind, I'm trying to be straight with

you. I've never confused genuine emotion with the sort of fixations some women get about men who have high-profile jobs. I know what I do cuts no ice with you—and I like that.'

'You do?' Better to be a fraud, she decided, than admit to him how often she'd walked away from one of his movies happily fantasising like most of the female audience.

'Of course I do.' He suddenly let go of her and rubbed his fingers distractedly through his dark hair. 'I'm not suggesting we leap into bed.'

Lindy swayed slightly. She'd wanted him to let her go yet now he had she felt oddly bereft. 'You're not?' She'd been under the impression that that was exactly what he'd been suggesting. Her delinquent mind had already examined several ways he might achieve this object. 'Why not? What's wrong with me?' Her hands went up to cover her mouth. 'I don't believe I said that!'

Sam's eyes sparkled with laughter and some of the tension seemed to drain from his body. 'Quite a lot, but nothing terminal,' he soothed. 'I thought we might get to know one another.'

'Fine,' she said tightly.

I'm ready to take a leap blindly into the dark and he wants to talk sport, hobbies and politics! she thought. It was mortifying to realise that she'd been his for the taking but he hadn't bothered. This puts things painfully in perspective, she thought bitterly.

'You want me now.' His heavily lashed eyes were watching her closely. 'Because you want the decision taken out of your hands.'

She shot him a startled look. 'That's not...' she began in a choked voice, wishing she didn't have to listen to the voice of caution in her head, but could allow the strong sexual chemistry to drown out her fears. His observation had a painful element of truth in it.

'You were saying?' he drawled slowly as the denial shrivelled on her tongue. 'In the morning you'd be able to decide, quite comfortably, that this was all some momentary aberration. That I'd taken advantage of you at a vulnerable moment. After all, I'm a shallow, film-star stud. Isn't that what we do?' he drawled sarcastically.

'Why should you care what I feel like tomorrow?' she hit back. 'I suppose you're worried I won't carry on working for you.'

'Get real, Rosalind; there are plenty of doctors who'd jump at the opportunity to replace you,' he said scornfully. 'Maybe I don't give a damn what you feel like. Maybe I am shallow and egocentric! Maybe this is about what *I* want. Maybe I want more...' A compelling intensity that totally transfixed Lindy had entered his voice. 'Maybe I think the foundations of any relationship are important. If you want it to last.'

'And you want it to last?' She saw the shock in her voice suddenly mirrored on his face. He froze.

'Things are going awfully fast here,' he muttered, rubbing his hand over the faint growth of stubble on his chin, 'but I think I must be saying that.' He glared at her almost warily. 'You aggravate me to hell!' he said, half to himself. 'The honest truth is I find you fascinating, Rosalind Lacey, and not just on a sexual level. Although,' he added, with a sudden grin, 'that *is* a major factor!'

Lindy stared at him in disbelief. 'I think I need to sit down. Do you use this line often?' she enquired, more out of habit than conviction, as she weakly sank into a rattan chair. She caught hold of a cushion and hugged it to her chest.

'If all I wanted to do was bed you, I could have done that without any soul-searching,' he reminded her ruthlessly. 'I'm not some predator,' he snarled.

She winced as she looked up at him and saw his expression was dark with anger. Ironically, he looked exactly like what he was denying at that moment. A shiver of apprehension slid slowly down her spine. He was a man with strong passions—a dangerous man. He didn't live in the same world as her. Was getting involved with Sam Rourke the sort of thing a sensible girl did?

'What are you suggesting?' she asked quietly. She didn't want to know. She'd almost made an awful mistake and, ironically, Sam had stopped her. She *ought* to be making it very clear she wasn't interested in *anything* he might suggest. She ought to be repairing the great gaping hole in her defences.

'Friends, *loving* friends.' Lindy felt colour stain her skin as he emphasised the word. 'We let things develop with an open mind and see what happens. Any time one of us wants out—'

'We walk,' she finished. It sounded very reasonable; so why did she feel uneasy? Getting to know Sam would make her vulnerable. This fact screamed at her but she ignored it. She could cope, couldn't she? Could she finally trust her own judgement?

'With no hard feelings.'

'You mean no kiss-and-tell stories in the tabloids?' She shot him a challenging glare. He'd better not be suggesting that!

'If I'm any judge of character that will never be an issue.'

'Thank you—I think,' she said drily. 'So what do we do now?' I don't have to go anywhere, she reminded herself. This will all end in tears, Lindy, girl!

Considering one of the most sinfully desirable men in the world wanted to date her, Lindy felt a curious sense of anticlimax. Her body was still feeling cheated out of the lovemaking it had craved, the lovemaking it had anticipated.

'Doesn't all this—' she made a wide encompassing gesture '—lack a certain spontaneity?'

Why hadn't he let her assuage this gnawing, aching hunger? All she'd needed was to lose herself in the mindless oblivion that beckoned every time she looked at him. Now things were complicated—dangerous.

The phone began to ring shrilly before Sam had an opportunity to reply. Lindy's glare was filled with the ambivalence that churned in her stomach. She turned her back on him and went into the living room to pick up the receiver.

'Adam!' Delighted surprise filled her voice as she heard the familiar deep tones at the other end. Adam forestalled her query as to her sister's health and then proceeded to give her news that took her breath away.

Sam had followed her into the room and stood leaning his muscular frame against the wall. His eyes didn't leave Lindy's face as she had what appeared to be a very one-sided conversation. Whatever was being said made her face light up with sheer delight. His own expression grew almost sombre as he watched her. He felt an unexpected stab of jealousy for the person who could give her so much pleasure. He was gripped by a fierce determination to make Rosalind smile at him like that.

Lindy replaced the receiver and looked at him with a stunned expression. She gave a small, silly grin. 'That was Adam,' she said happily.

'Who the hell is Adam?' Sam growled the question that was uppermost in his mind.

'I told you, Adam is my brother-in-law,' Lindy said impatiently, hardly registering the aggression in his voice. 'Oh, Sam, Anna's having a baby—two babies actually. She's sick, but otherwise all right, Adam says. Isn't it *marvellous*!'

With a cry that was halfway between a laugh and a sob, she ran across the room and threw herself at the general area of his chest. Sam responded in the required fashion and lifted her bodily into his arms with crushing enthusiasm.

'It sure feels pretty marvellous to me,' he agreed. 'Why are you crying?'

'I'm so happy.'

'Stupid question,' he said, sliding the damp strands of her pale hair from the side of her face and tucking them behind her ear.

'What are you doing?' Lindy asked in a dazed fashion as he began to stride out of the room with her in his arms.

'I'm being spontaneous,' he said, with a very devilish grin. '*Very* spontaneous.' She felt a rumble of satisfaction in his chest as he kicked open a bedroom door with unnecessary force.

'What about getting to know one another?'

Sam laid her carefully down on his bed. 'One of the first things you'll learn about me is that I'm subject to violent mood swings and I have a habit of overestimating my endurance. I prefer to call it adapting to a change in circumstances,' he explained smoothly. The expression in his eyes made her shudder as an answering primitive hunger jolted through her body.

'It's as well to know the worst,' she said breathlessly as he deftly untied the belt of her robe.

His mouth silenced any further observations with ruthless efficiency.

CHAPTER FOUR

LINDY lay in the gathering darkness, unable to sleep even though her body was weary. The night was sultry and the curtains pulled across the open window barely stirred in the stillness. The man beside her moved.

His features were a blur in the dark. The thin sheet skimmed his hips, leaving his powerful torso exposed. Lindy ran her fingers lightly down the curve of his powerful shoulder, over his hair-sprinkled chest to the flat hardness of his belly. The layer of sweat that had recently covered his skin had evaporated and his skin had a marvellous satiny texture. She stilled her exploration as he shifted in his sleep once more, drawing closer to her.

It wasn't a dream, it was real. For better or worse Sam Rourke was her lover. As if to convince herself it was real, her mind kept replaying recent events.

His mouth had barely seemed to leave hers, but somehow he had accomplished the complicated removal of her damp swimsuit before she had even realised it. The memory of the greedy growl that had reverberated in his throat as he'd knelt above her and looked long and slowly at her naked form made her stomach muscles flutter almost as much as they had at the time.

Sensible Dr Lacey would have been alarmed at the primitive expression of desire that had blazed in his magnificent eyes, but Lindy had felt a swell of reckless anticipation. Her body had felt so sensitised by his survey that she'd almost imagined electrical currents were running under her skin.

'You are beautiful,' he'd gasped rawly.

'I haven't done this for a long time.' It was something she'd had to get out of the way then whilst she was still capable.

'How long?'

'Long.' She pushed aside memories she didn't want. It was marvellously easy when Sam filled her thoughts.

'Then we'll have to make this worth the wait, won't we?' he murmured silkily.

Lindy nodded in silent agreement as he lowered his frame onto the bed beside her. His touch was tantalisingly soft as he moved over her body. With a moan she lifted her head and dragged his face to her own.

'Kiss me!' she demanded fiercely. His lips were only a breath away—the musky, male odour of him filled her nostrils. She wanted to fill her senses with him. The roar of blood thundering in her temples was deafening.

The force of his mouth as it plundered her own pressed her back deep into the pillow. Her body felt fluid as she wrapped her arms around his neck and, back arched, pressed closer to him. When he lifted his head her breathing was wildly erratic.

'You're *so* beautiful,' she panted as his tongue flicked over the graceful curve of her throat.

'You love me for my face?' His voice was thick and muffled as his hands explored the rounded contours of her breasts.

'I think the rest of you might be passable too, only it's difficult to tell right now—' A sharp gasp cut off her words. Sam's lips had closed around one pink ruched bud. The sensation as he suckled fiercely sent her out of control. She was burning up and Sam had lit the fire!

She slid her hands over his shoulders and made contact with his skin. She made a small guttural sound of satisfaction. Urgently, she moved her hands lower down his back. There was the sound of fabric tearing and he lifted his head sharply.

With an abrupt, jerky motion he rose to his knees and began fumbling with his shirt buttons. Lindy found his unsteady efforts far more exciting than the beautifully lit, choreographed slickness of his love scenes on film. With a soft curse he pulled at the garment, sending the remaining buttons flying in several directions. This wasn't soft-focus lovemaking—this was urgent and primal.

Tongue caught between her teeth, Lindy reached up to unfasten the buckle on his leather belt. She shot him hot, furtive glances from under the fringe of her lashes as she pulled the denim apart. Using the leverage of her fingers in his waistband, she hoisted herself up from the bed until her tight, tingling breasts were pressed against the warm, hard flesh of his belly.

The strength quite abruptly drained from her body, and if Sam hadn't wrapped one powerful arm around her middle at the critical moment she'd have slid bonelessly back against the covers.

'I'm shaking,' she whispered.

'That makes two of us.' His smile caressed and beguiled her.

'Well, I hope you can manage the rest of your clothes because my co-ordination has taken a holiday.' Her smouldering glance moved over his face as if it were tasting him. At least her eyes couldn't leave any marks. Best not to risk the ire of a production company. The thought wrenched a small bubble of laughter from her throat.

'What's so funny?' he asked throatily. He pushed his free hand into her hair and inclined her head towards him. The gift of her throat proved too much to resist. With a hoarse moan he bent over and tasted the salty flavour of her creamy, flawless skin. As his mouth slid lower so did they, until she lay supine, shadowed by his protective bulk.

She felt a moment's agitation when he raised himself up onto his knees and distanced himself from her. The blip in her bliss was only momentary as he proved that, even if he was afflicted by the shakes, he was more than capable of removing his clothing.

Her languorous glance slid slowly and deliberately from his face. He reacted with pulsing awareness to her eyes, as if their touch were real. The thought of actually touching the silky, sheathed hardness made her draw a voluptuous, shuddering sigh.

'Have mercy, lover; this is meant to be sweet and slow.' He lowered his body down to cover her thigh to thigh, hard muscle to soft, yielding flesh.

'What if I feel urgent and greedy?' She spoke into his ear and curled her fingers into the dense springiness of his luxuriant hair. The weight of him, the glorious strength of his awesome body felt so good.

'Then a last-minute change of direction might be arranged.'

Her tongue sought the pulse spot at the base of his throat and a deep shudder rippled through his powerful frame. Memory told her she'd always been a passive partner in the dim and distant past. Discovering the unexpected delights of feminine power made her feel feverish and dizzy.

'God, Sam, I think I'm out of control,' she confessed raggedly against his damp skin.

'The grooves you're gouging in my back sort of give the game away.' Despite the ambiguous cocktail of warmth and ferocity in his voice, the fingers that opened the foil wrapper were steady.

His gentle probing of her most sensitive regions initiated a series of agonised pleas for release. The tormenting stroke of his fingers stopped long enough for him to anchor her thrashing head and look deep into her feverish eyes.

'I want to watch you.' And he did, the violet-blue of his eyes almost obliterated by his dilated pupils. The possessive exultation she saw there made Lindy want to shout out loud to release the explosion of pure joy she felt. She wasn't entirely sure that she hadn't done just that!

Feeling the probing touch of his manhood against her own slick heat, Lindy eagerly wrapped her long pale legs around him. The anchor was complete as he slid smoothly into her.

Her initial response was uncontrolled and fierce, but gradually she was swamped and absorbed by the delicate rhythm Sam slowly built up.

'That's it, sweetheart, don't rush, hold on,' Sam encouraged her hoarsely. He dug deeply into his reserves of self-control so as not to respond immediately to the thunderous roar in his blood. He didn't want his own greed to spoil the special moment. The delicate balance of his control slipped when Lindy reached up and suckled one pebble-flat male nipple. With a harsh cry he plunged deeper into her welcoming heat and brought them both to a ferocious, gasping climax.

'What are you thinking about?'

'You.' Turning her head to meet the sleepy, sexy stare, Lindy didn't have time to wonder whether the truth might inflate his ego to unmanageable proportions.

'Fascinating subject.'

'Smug, egotistical—' She broke off, laughing as he hooked one arm underneath her and, one hand firmly curved around her behind, shifted her onto her side. The gurgle of amusement faded as she found herself nose to nose with him.

'You were saying?' he murmured, watching her from under the sweep of those ludicrously long lashes.

'You're delicious,' she said. It wasn't a situation where defences or half-truths would do.

'Delicious?' He queried her use of adjective with a quirk of his mobile lips.

'Uh-huh,' she confirmed. 'Like one of those delicious, sugary works of art it always seems criminal to eat.'

He closed his eyes and whistled softly. 'What a sinful picture.'

'What is?' she whispered, running her fingers over the hard curve of his angular jaw. Her touch met with the faint resistance of a slight covering of stubble. The sinfully suggestive surge of his body against her distracted Lindy from this fascinating discovery—everything about Sam was fascinating!

'That very pretty mouth nibbling me.'

She drew a sharp, startled gasp. 'Oh, my goodness!' Vivid images danced across her vision.

'My very thought,' he rumbled, amusement echoing in the vault of his chest. 'God, but I love you!' He was still laughing when he claimed her parted lips.

Lindy gave herself up to the spiralling excitement. She wouldn't read anything into a term which people around her seemed to use with reckless abandon. Like a missing piece in a jigsaw, something clicked in her brain. It was easy to blot out the truth when her senses were filled with the taste, touch and smell of Sam.

'Sweet and slow this time?' His voice was warm and rich with anticipation.

'It sounds fine to me,' she agreed faintly.

It was.

'Well, what do you think?'

He sounded as if he really cared about her opinion. 'I think she's beautiful, Sam.' That he loved every gleaming inch of the forty-eight-foot boat had been obvious as he'd shown her over the *Jennifer*, his pride concealed behind an endearingly offhand manner.

He seemed to relax a little after scrutinising her expression with a strange intensity. Lindy had the feeling she'd passed some sort of test.

'We'll motor out to sea and then you can feel what sail power is all about,' he promised.

Sam's enthusiasm was infectious, but all the same the feeling of raw power when the white sails unfurled filled her with a totally unexpected sense of awe and delight.

She wasn't alone long before Sam came to join her. Not used to the pitch of the deck, she caught hold of his arm to steady herself as she took the few steps to his side.

'It's incredible,' she shouted, laughing up at him. Exhilaration sparkled in her eyes.

'It's home,' he said simply. 'Nothing else gives the same sense of freedom.' His blue eyes were fixed on the distant horizon.

Lindy frowned; for a moment his abstraction alienated her. He was so totally at home in this environment. She shrugged to banish the transitory feeling. She didn't want anything to spoil the day. She had him all to herself. Work occupied such a lot of Sam's energy and she'd been anticipating these two days with impatient delight. Now it was here she wanted the time to last for ever. She was glad that Hope had refused Sam's invitation to join them, and she hoped she had hidden her unsisterly chagrin at the casual inclusion.

The ever present worry that Sam Rourke was an addiction she was going to find hard to break when the time came surfaced, only to be banished once more to the back of her mind. She saw him every day on set, but his behaviour there gave no hint of their private relationship. Whilst she didn't want to be the object of gossip and conjecture, sometimes Lindy did find the situation frustrating. When she listened to yet another speculative comment about whom Sam might be seeing she wanted to scream, No, it's not her, it's me he's with! She would stop short, shocked by the thoughts in her head. It was as if they belonged to a stranger.

Content to ride the white-crested waves in silence, she leant back against him. For the first time in days the tension that had lain coiled just below the surface was absent from his body. He was pushing himself, if not to the limit—because she already knew his endurance was formidable—pushing himself hard. Lindy traced a pattern with her rope-soled shoe on the teak deck. No rich man's plaything, this craft. Sam had made it quite plain that this was a working yacht, a steel-hulled ketch capable of crossing oceans.

Everything below deck was neat and functional. The craftsmanship in the oak fittings was superb, but there were no flamboyant touches. The electronic gadgetry was state-of-the-art, but other than that the fittings had a spartan touch. Sam Rourke was not all he appeared on the surface.

He looked comically alarmed when Lindy offered to prepare lunch in the small galley.

'Don't worry,' she responded, not rising to the bait. 'The most ambitious thing I intend doing is slicing bread and tossing a salad. We can't all be culinary geniuses.'

'Your talents lie in quite different directions, Doctor,' he leered. Lindy yelped as the hand aimed at her behind made contact.

'You're disgusting,' she scolded, a smile on her lips as she disappeared below deck.

'You wouldn't have me any other way.' The chuckled retort followed her descent.

She hummed as she worked in the small galley. The last three weeks had been the most exhilarating she could ever remember. Despite being plagued by doubts and subject to wild mood swings which were alien to her nature, she wouldn't have altered the series of events which had made her this man's lover.

Half an hour later, laden with a tray, Lindy made her way up onto the deck. Sam took the tray from her hands. 'I'm impressed,' he said.

'You're supposed to be.'

In a companionable silence they ate the cold meats, salad and crusty fresh bread.

'More?' Sam held up the half-empty bottle of Chardonnay.

'I'd better not—too much sea air and wine and I'll be asleep.

'Do you always sail alone?' she asked, flopping back on the plaid rug and shading her eyes against the sun.

'Not today.'

'You know what I mean.'

'Usually. I enjoy the illusion of freedom. I decide where I go and when. The only responsibility I have is staying alive. The elements have a way of putting life in perspective.'

She rolled on her stomach and cradled her chin in her hands. 'What happened to Sam Rourke international superstar, with his fancy cars, glitzy clubs and glitzier girlfriends?'

'I hope the public are a little more open-minded when I slip out of character than you are.'

'I didn't mean that,' she hastily shot back. She levered herself to her knees and placed her palms on his thighs, just above where the frayed edges of his cut-off denims exposed his hair-roughened flesh. 'I just find it difficult to reconcile the Sam Rourke I know with the one in the glossy magazines. I wake up at night and wonder what on earth Sam Rourke sees in me. I like this Sam,' she admitted huskily. 'I like him a lot.'

There was a silence. Lindy chewed her lip; she wished

she could see his face, but the sun was in her eyes. Her heart was thudding with trepidation. Their relationship had been warm and loving. They laughed a lot and made love even more, but Lindy was well aware that this was a thing that existed in the present—it had no foundation and no future.

Though it gave her pain, Lindy accepted this because she loved him. She ought to have censored the comments that had come straight from the heart before they'd reached her mouth. Would he withdraw from her, back off?

'Sometimes I wonder. You seem so detached at times...' The breath was crushed from her ribs as he hauled her up across his lap. His expression behind the rakish grin held a strong element of triumph. Lindy's arms curled around his neck and for the first time she allowed herself to hope the unthinkable! Perhaps they did have some sort of future together?

'You know me, I don't gush.' The quirk of his lips showed that he too recalled the comment she'd made the day they met.

'How could I forget?' The smile faded from his eyes as he brushed back the strands of hair from her face. 'I don't really know you at all, do I? Though what I do know I like.'

He could charm snowflakes from a blue sky, she knew that, but with her he didn't try to. He wasn't trying to crowd or rush her with sweet words. He was letting her set her own pace. Lindy recognised his wariness for what it was because she too felt the same way. 'I could say the same.' The past was suddenly a great gulf between them. Could she ever share her past with anyone, even Sam?

'I've missed you this last week—since I moved back on board *Jennifer*,' he said.

Lindy's smile was redolent of satisfaction. 'I hardly

noticed you were gone,' she lied. Amazingly, Hope hadn't made any comment when Sam's stay at the cottage had extended beyond the original few days.

'Liar,' he breathed softly. The kiss beside her mouth was a sweet-scented whisper. 'Ned seems quite taken with you.'

'Ned?'

'Nice guy, writer, good-looking if you discount the moustache he's trying to grow. Have a heart, Rosalind; the guy follows you with his eyes like a faithful spaniel.'

'Of course I know who Ned is.'

'He asked me if I thought he stood a chance with you.'

'He did what?' She'd found him friendly and helpful, but it hadn't occurred to her for one minute that he imagined...

'Do I have to spell it out? He's lusting after you.'

'What did you say? Did you tell him...?' she began in alarm. She hoped she hadn't been giving off any false signals.

A spasm of anger twisted his features. Though why he should be annoyed because she didn't want to advertise their relationship she couldn't imagine. He was the one who took care not to broadcast the situation. In her darker moments she imagined it was because she wasn't the sort of female who was good for his image. She was always ashamed of these persistent thoughts, because she knew that Sam wasn't either vain or superficial.

'What do you think I said?' he bit back. 'You don't stand a chance because the lady is sleeping in my bed. At least she would be if I had my way.'

'You're the one who thought things were going fast.' He made it sound as though this was a bone of contention between them, she thought indignantly.

'I didn't say I didn't like it that way,' he pointed out pedantically.

She gave a small grunt of irritation. 'What did you say to poor Ned?' she persisted.

' "Poor" Ned,' he repeated, shaking his head. 'A man dreads that prefix,' he intoned solemnly. 'It's so maternal. Roughly translated, it says, You don't stand a chance, you poor slob.'

'I'll sit on you if you don't answer me!' she threatened.

'Promises, promises. OK, OK,' he conceded, shielding his head from her fists with his brown forearms. 'I was gentle and tactful.'

'That would have been a first.'

'But I wasn't encouraging.'

Something in his expression made her do a doubletake. 'Were you jealous?' she asked incredulously.

Sam shrugged, but didn't deny it, much to Lindy's secret delight. 'For all I knew you might be secretly lusting after him. A man doesn't like to hear from another guy how gorgeous the woman he's sleeping with is. How great her legs are, or how kind she is to children and animals. I think I showed great restraint, but I made it clear you were heavily involved with another.'

'You deserve a badge. Did you say "heavily"?'

' "Heavily" is what I said,' he confirmed. 'And a badge is not what I deserve,' he growled.

The musky masculine odour of his body made her toes curl and wrenched a deep, shuddering sigh from her lips. 'Don't you need to steer or anything?' she gasped as his fingers slid under the cropped top she was wearing.

'I've been thinking about this all week,' he groaned. The dark, sultry look in his eyes as he rolled her onto her back and came to rest on top of her made Lindy's stomach do several backward flips.

'Then why did you invite Hope along?' She couldn't prevent the pique from entering her voice.

'My dear, darling Rosalind.' Laughing, he stripped the

thin top from her unresisting body. 'I was going through polite motions. Hope wouldn't have been indiscreet enough to say yes.'

'You think she *knows*?' Rosalind tried to get up but a large hand on her ribcage prevented her.

'Hasn't she warned you about my reputation?'

'In a roundabout manner,' Lindy recalled with a frown. 'She hasn't been around much and I thought we were being very discreet…' Her voice trailed off as he laughed again. 'I'm only thinking of you,' she complained. 'You obviously want to keep this a secret.'

'I don't care if the world knows how I feel about you.'

'You don't?' I wish he'd share it with me, she thought, seething with frustration. His expression was impossible to interpret and it would be a fatal error to read what she wanted to hear into his words.

'Enough said on the subject.'

Not nearly enough for her.

He seemed to read the bafflement in her face. 'I don't volunteer personal material for public consumption. You have to draw a line somewhere or they'd eat you up alive,' he elaborated. 'Worse still, *I* might start to believe all the publicity hype. I've known people who do and, believe me, it's a pathetic sight. Don't get me wrong, I'm not precious enough to bad-mouth the media—they've got their job to do, and I often reap the benefits. I play the game, but they're my rules. Photo opportunities are one thing, but you won't find one of me on this deck.

'The studio can leak as many fictional stories as they like about me and my latest leading lady. I'll even pose for the photos—but they won't get a picture of me with you. I'll do the rounds and publicise this film, but at the end of the day what I do, and with whom, is my business.' The sobriety of his expression was broken by a sudden wicked grin. 'At least we don't have to worry about tele-photo lenses out here.'

'There's probably a satellite somewhere up there.' She dreamily sketched a wide arc above her head. 'Someone, somewhere is watching us.' She tried to match his casual humour, but the ferocity of his provocative stare as it roamed over her half-clad figure was too distracting to resist. Her skin tingled with anticipation of his masterly touch.

'Let them look! I don't need any help to remember exactly how you look now in the sunlight. I'm making a complete mental inventory so I can compare it to how you'll look later, when I make love to you under the moon.'

'You're planning on doing that?' She reached up and grasped his firm buttocks in her hands. She had no intention of playing hard to get, not when the erotic promise in his voice had her shaking with feverish desire.

'A lot depends on your co-operation,' he admitted huskily.

'I might be persuaded...' Her words were lost in the warm recesses of his mouth.

It wasn't as warm now and Lindy had retreated to the cabin to pull on a cotton sweater over her shirt. She'd spent the last hour in the cockpit and her head was spinning with nautical terms. Sam had assured her that the technology took all the hard work out of navigation, but she had other thoughts on the subject.

When she returned to the cockpit Lindy could tell immediately from his expression that something was wrong. The smile faded from her face.

'I've been talking to the coastguard. The storm front they were expecting tomorrow night is ahead of schedule.'

'What does that mean?' She tried to hide the disappointment that bit deep.

'It means I have to take you ashore tonight. I'll take her south of the point before it gets too rough to chance navigating the bar. She'll be sheltered from the worst of it there.'

'Do we have to?' Lindy could hardly believe the faint tremor in her voice. From Sam's sharp look he had heard it too. God, don't go all clinging and pathetic on him, Lindy, girl, she told herself. 'Would you if you were alone?' she asked in a more self-possessed tone.

'I'm not alone; I've got a priceless cargo to consider.'

It took her a few seconds to realise what he meant. A flush of pleasure washed over her skin. 'I'm sorry if I've spoilt it for you.' The way he was looking at her made her feel precious and cherished. The experience was novel and strangely satisfying. Men didn't, as a rule, feel the need to cherish Lindy. She appeared far too capable and cool to incite such chivalrous responses.

Sam took her chin in his fingers. 'You haven't spoilt anything for me.' His stare was deeply compelling. 'Sure, I'm disappointed, but there will be plenty of other times.'

There would! She could feel herself glowing with pleasure. Any smuggler and I'll start purring, she thought, startled by the strength of her own response. 'Won't a landlubber like me cramp your style?'

'I was a landlubber once myself.'

'You were?' She was genuinely shocked; the sea seemed very much his natural environment. She'd assumed he'd inherited the knowledge—he seemed to belong. His lithe body moved over the heaving boat in a sure-footed and natural manner which she envied and loved to watch.

'Sure. I hail from land-locked Ohio. I'm a farm boy. I first stepped on a boat when I was nineteen. I got work on the coast, in the docks. One day they were doing a photo shoot on a yacht in the bay. A group of us stayed after work to watch, heckle a bit and watch the babes.' His ironic, self-deprecating grin flashed out. 'The guy who was meant to be modelling kept turning green every time they cast off. For some reason the woman who was in charge of the shoot grabbed me and I thought, What the hell? I already had my shirt off, and it couldn't be that hard to smile at a camera! Please don't tell Hope I said that or she'll have my hide. I was only nineteen, with all the arrogance of youth.'

'Some things never change.' Lindy could almost visualise the bold-eyed, bronzed, bare-chested youth he had been. Sam might wonder why the woman had selected him, but she didn't!

Sam just grinned in response. 'I ended up on the inside spread of some glossy and I got my first taste of a deck under my feet. The photos led to a part in a TV show, and the rest, as they say, is history. I bought *Jennifer* with the proceeds of my first film.' His eyes rose towards her masts.

These confidences gave Lindy food for thought. She had assumed that Sam had a privileged background, but this information made it very clear that wasn't the case. She hoped she was reading the signals right and he really was as serious as she was, because the more he let her see of the real Sam Rourke, the deeper she was falling! The old Rosalind would have cut her losses and run to save herself from possible heartache. The new Rosalind was going to see it through to the bitter end, no matter what the outcome!

Sam made her wear a safety harness on the journey back. It was a good habit to get into, he said, when you sailed solo. Lindy might be a novice but Sam's manoeuvres in the rapidly worsening conditions, to avoid the sand bar just visible under the wild white spray, looked impressive.

Lindy slept for most of the hour's car journey back to Hope's cottage. She woke up as they negotiated the rough track leading up to the small scatter of houses, and was still rubbing her eyes when Sam's exclamation of anger brought her fully awake.

She peered out of the window to see what had brought the thunderous expression to his face. The rough parking area outside the cottage was crammed with vehicles and a mill of people, some bearing camera and sound equipment, were jostling to reach the crowded veranda.

'Stay here!' Sam's expression was grim as he pulled the four-wheel drive up behind a startlingly flashy red limousine. He banged the car with his hand. 'Dallas! I might have guessed!'

Lindy didn't even consider following this peremptory order. There had been none of the gentle lover left in his brief glance. Sam had already donned his professional director persona.

She might easily have been invisible for all the notice anyone took of her, but Sam's presence created an immediate impression.

'Sam—Sam Rourke—did you know about Lacey and Lloyd? How long has it been going on?'

'Sam, have you been covering for the lovers? Are you personally involved with Lacey?'

'Is it true you *and* Lloyd have been living with Lacey?'

'Is it true Lloyd only put up the money for your venture on the understanding Lacey got the lead?'

Sam shouldered his way through the pressed figures and ignored the cries from all sides. He disregarded the microphones shoved in his face with the ease of long practice. Lindy followed in his broad-shouldered wake before the bodies closed in behind him.

For the first time Lindy appreciated the extent of Hope's acting ability. Her sister stood, a still, calm figure, smiling benignly at the chaos around her. Her face was free of make-up and, wearing a white tee shirt and bleached denims, she was a stark contrast to the female who stood opposite. The glowing natural appearance versus the painted, sexy siren look. Which one did men prefer? Lindy mused, staring at the tableau before her. Who could tell with men? Which did Sam favour?

'Sam!' The dramatic rich contralto tones alerted anyone who hadn't known that he was there. The bosom which overflowed from the laced red velvet heaved effectively. 'I can't believe you're part of this conspiracy.'

Sam took a comprehensive assessment of the situation in one swift glance. 'Hello, Dallas,' he said drily. 'Travelling light today, I see.'

Lindy, caught up in the press of bodies, couldn't catch the words but it was obvious from their body language that these two knew one another.

The brown eyes of the singer narrowed in amused appreciation, none of which was apparent when she spoke. 'I want the world to know what a cold-hearted, conniving little bitch this husband-stealer is!' Her contemptuous glance flicked over Lacey.

Lindy gave a gasp of anger and watched incredulously as her sister remained totally impassive. She'd expected to see the sexy siren laid out cold, but no, Hope just stood there with that sphinx-like smile on her lips.

'I think they've got the idea now,' Sam said. The glint of anger in his eyes was a warning. 'When's the new album out, Dallas?' he asked, in a soft aside none of the listening ears could catch. 'I think you've had enough free publicity for one day, don't you?'

Dallas laughed, throwing back her head and shaking back her mane of unexpectedly red hair. 'Dear Sam, don't worry, I'm about done here. I think she owes me this. *I* like to be the one to walk away from a man.'

There was genuine vitriol in her glance as she looked towards Hope. 'I almost feel sorry for you, you talentless clothes-horse.' Her trained voice reached every ear which had been trying, with seething frustration, to hear what the two stars were saying. 'There are thousands of little tramps out there who can act flat on their backs, honey. In a few years' time you'll be yesterday's news and I'll still have my voice. Don't expect Lloyd to be around to dry your tears because you haven't got what it takes to hold his interest.'

You could have heard a pin drop.

'Neither, it seems, have you.'

Lindy wanted to applaud as her sister turned and, stately as a queen, retreated inside the cottage. Unhappy at not having the last word, Dallas flung a lengthy monologue of unladylike insults at the unresponsive wooden panels until Sam leant over and said something.

Whatever it was it had the desired effect. Dallas turned and paused gracefully for the clicking shutters before retreating, flanked by two large bodyguards. Lindy found herself suddenly eye to eye with the woman. A wave of overpowering perfume preceded her and Lindy let her distaste show on her face. The singer's brown eyes narrowed as she saw it.

'And who might you be?'

'How dare you speak to my sister like that?' Lindy's voice might not be trained to carry, but her posture was enough to tell the eager audience the show wasn't over yet.

'Rosalind, leave it.' Sam shouldered his way to her side.

She was too angry to hear the warning in his voice. She shrugged at the restraining hand on her shoulder.

'My sister has more integrity in her little finger than the whole pack of you put together!'

The brown eyes swept with amusement over the slim figure clad in chinos and a cotton sweater. Lindy's cheeks, coloured to the lightest of honey shades by several weeks in the sun, were flushed with temper. The soft blue of her eyes had been replaced by a stormy grey.

'Is this one yours, Sam?' One pencilled brow rose in amused condescension that made Lindy's blood boil.

'Cut it out, Dallas,' Sam snapped. 'Come on, Rosalind. The show is over, guys.'

Lindy spun around and glared furiously at him. Who did he think he was anyway? Telling her what to do!

'Are you Lacey's sister?' Flashes of light blinded and disorientated her. 'What is your relationship with Sam?'

Lindy held up her hand to shield her eyes. She no longer fought Sam's attempts to get her back to the house. It occurred to her, too late, that she'd only made matters worse.

'Where do you live, Rosalind?'

'Here—I live here,' she mumbled. The crowd of bodies pressed around them was oppressive. The whole scene was approaching nightmarish proportions.

'You live here with the two of them, Sam, is that right? How cosy.' A nerve was ticking away in Sam's lean jaw as he faced down the heavy-set reporter who blocked their path with his bulk. 'Was Rosalind included?' The insinuating smile he cast in her direction made Lindy feel sick. 'Was she included in the deal when Lloyd financed the film? I can't say I blame you...' He got no further before Sam's right fist shot out and floored him.

Sam turned to Lindy, lifted her fireman fashion over one shoulder, and strode to the door which was opened by a wide-eyed Hope and swiftly bolted behind them.

Hope looked silently from a grim-faced Sam to her

sister, still hoisted over his shoulder, her fair hair flopping in her eyes. Laughter suddenly doubled her up and she slid to the floor, her back braced against the door.

'Oh, boy, oh, boy…' Hope moaned as the tears poured down her cheeks. 'Lloyd always says he doesn't know anyone who plays the media as well as Sam Rourke. He's so…he's so unflappable and controlled!' Storms of giggles broke out again. 'You upstaged Dallas; she'll never forgive you.'

Outside, the floored reporter picked himself up. 'Jeez,' he said, rubbing his jaw. A look of unholy joy spread slowly across his face. 'Did you get that, Pete?' he yelled, looking around for his photographer.

'Sure I got that,' his colleague confirmed, 'but so did everyone else.'

'I've got something they haven't.'

'What's that?'

'Bruises!'

CHAPTER FIVE

AN HOUR after the last reporter had departed, Lindy joined Sam and Hope where they sat, talking in subdued tones, at the table. Fresh from the shower, she was wearing a striped towelling robe. She tucked her wet hair behind her ears and sat down.

'Feeling better now?' her sister enquired sympathetically.

Lindy nodded. The other two, she reflected, seemed to have coped with the experience a lot better than she had. She'd felt grubby and shaken by the whole nightmarish encounter. She reached out to take the coffee cup Hope handed her; at least her hands were steady now.

'Want some?'

Lindy shook her head and watched with surprise as her sister glugged some spirit from the whisky bottle into her own cup. Perhaps, she reflected, she'd underestimated her sister's response to the incident. It made her feel a little less inadequate to discover Hope wasn't quite as invulnerable as she made out.

'You get used to it,' said Sam.

Lindy wasn't sure whether this remark was addressed to her or Hope, or perhaps both of them. 'I'm not sure I want to.'

'It's fatal to let them needle you and lose your temper.'

He's telling *me* that? Lindy widened her eyes and stared at him.

Sam had the grace to look self-conscious, but a stubborn light gleamed in his eyes. 'The slob deserved it.' His nostrils flared and his jaw tightened. 'When he started pawing you...' he recalled, from between gritted teeth.

Actually he'd only touched her arm, but Lindy wisely didn't correct him. Had it just been a matter of the final straw that had evoked his response? Or did Sam's feelings really run as deep as it seemed where she was concerned? she wondered wistfully.

Get real, Lindy, she told herself firmly. Get a firm hold on your imagination. Sam had never said anything to give her the impression he wanted anything more than a brief affair. She could still distinctly recall every word he'd said about casual affairs and film sets. She reminded herself of them frequently, just to keep her feet on the ground. They were both free to walk; he'd made that clear. The problem, she thought, is I don't want to walk!

Why did you do it, Sam? Do you love me? I love you. For an awful moment she thought she'd actually said the words that kept going round and round in her head. When he looked directly at her she flushed darkly and turned to her sister.

'Are you going to tell us what this is all about?' she said, a lot more sharply than she'd intended. 'What *is* going on between you and Lloyd? I notice *he* wasn't here when you needed him!'

Hope looked miserably from her sister to Sam. 'I promised not to tell anyone, but I suppose...'

'You better had suppose,' Lindy said indignantly. 'One thing's certain,' she added darkly, 'you're not leaving this table until you've spilled the beans.'

Hope gave a rueful grin. 'I think Sam's already guessed...'

'Some,' he confirmed.

'Lucky him,' Lindy said, casting a resentful glare in his direction.

Hope rested her elbows on the table and positioned

her chin on her steepled fingers. 'Lloyd is leaving Dallas—but not for me. Lloyd is in love—but not with me,' she explained wearily. 'He and Shirley—Shirley in Continuity; you know her?'

Lindy nodded. Nothing could astound her after today. Shirley, she could vaguely recall, was a woman in her late thirties with brown hair and a nice smile. When she screwed up her face to draw a mental image, Lindy had a general impression of serenity. Nobody could be more different from the dazzling Dallas!

'They've been seeing one another for nearly a year now,' Hope continued. 'Lloyd and Dallas had been living their separate lives for ages before that. Lloyd predicted pretty much how Dallas would react, and he doesn't much care—you know Lloyd, hide like a rhino—but there's a problem. Shirley has a stepson.'

'That's a problem?' Lindy began sarcastically. Why didn't Hope just get to the point?

'Shirley's stepson is in politics, Rosalind.' Sam took up the story as Hope glared at her impatient sibling. 'He's up for appointment to a very prestigious post. There's some opposition to him and any breath of scandal could scupper his chances.'

'So you've been a diversion, and *you've* known all along,' she accused Sam, rounding on him furiously. It's great to know how much everyone trusts me! she thought bitterly.

'Not really, but as you were such an excellent advocate of Hope's moral fibre I looked around for an alternative explanation. The only way anything made sense was if Hope was acting as a smokescreen. I mean, Lloyd may not be the most subtle guy in the world, but he was rubbing everyone's nose in the fact he was supposedly having a hot affair with Hope, and it just didn't ring true. What he was laying a smokescreen for, and why, I didn't know until just now.'

'You're both sworn to secrecy,' Hope said anxiously.

'As if I'd go blabbing!' Lindy cried indignantly. 'You might have trusted me—I've been worried sick. I think Lloyd has used you shamefully!'

'A bit of gossip never hurt anyone,' Hope said with a grin. Despite her brisk denial, Lindy could see the lines of strain around her mouth. 'Besides, the truth will come out in a few weeks and it won't matter. I'll ring Mum and Dad in the morning to warn them before the dirt hits the papers back home. I know how much they'll hate it.' She gave an anguished frown.

'They'll understand,' Lindy responded with sympathy.

'That's the problem—they *always* understand. It makes me feel an absolute rat. Why couldn't we have harsh and unpleasant parents?' she asked with an ironical smile. 'It'd be so much easier to let them down. Unconditional love is the very devil to live up to. I'm dead beat. Does anyone mind if I turn in?'

'She's feeling the pressure,' Lindy said anxiously as the door closed behind her sister.

'She'll cope. She's tough.'

'You're heartless.' She rounded on him.

'And you're her sister, not her *mother*!' Sam responded with brutal frankness.

This comment wiped what little colour she had from her cheeks. The bruised expression in her eyes made him reach across and catch her small, cold hands between his. 'What did I say?' he asked in bewilderment.

'Nothing…nothing,' she denied, shaking her head. For a moment she almost told him. The sordid past nearly came tumbling out. She just couldn't bear to see the distaste on his face. Besides, it wasn't the sort of thing you went telling someone you probably wouldn't see again in a few weeks. It wasn't as if their professional lives were likely to cross again. Working on the film set had been an experience, but Lindy was anxious to get back to what she did best.

'I think you and Hope should move out of here.'

'Why?' His words brought her back to the present with a jolt.

'Now the media know you're here you'll never have any peace. I'll talk to Lloyd. Under the circumstances, I think he should offer you sanctuary behind his security-guard-patrolled, ten-foot-high perimeter fence. The place he's rented for the duration is like Fort Knox.' He gave a decisive nod, narrowing his eyes as he considered the situation. 'Yeah, that's the best thing all round. He's back from LA later tonight—I'd better bring him up to speed. I'll get to him before the press do.'

'It sounds awful,' Lindy objected. 'A prison! Will all this affect the film?'

'A very luxurious prison,' Sam assured her drily. 'And you can be sure of no nasty surprises like today's. As for the movie, there's some truth to the old maxim that there's no such thing as bad publicity.'

Lindy wasn't fooled by the words; she could see his sharp mind was still weighing the repercussions of today. If she'd held her tongue he would never have got directly involved. He certainly wouldn't have punched anyone! It was bound to affect their relationship if this had a detrimental effect on the film, she thought miserably.

'You're not staying here tonight, then?' She swallowed the awful sense of loss which abruptly threatened to overwhelm her.

'I don't think that would be a good idea.' His azure gaze moved over her averted profile, but his attention seemed elsewhere.

'Fine,' she replied lightly. She wasn't about to beg. She had some pride left! He could have asked her to move in with him on the yacht. The fact he hadn't said a lot about the situation!

'I can see why Hope needs protecting,' she persisted stubbornly. 'But why do I have to go? I could stay here.'

'After my performance out there?' he scoffed. 'You're not that naive, Rosalind! You know what people are going to be saying.'

Stung by the fact he was leaving, and that she had a humiliating impulse to beg him to take her along, Lindy snarled sarcastically at him. 'And *what* will they be saying? I'm not psychic!' She had a sudden image of herself clinging to one of his long legs as he strode along, oblivious. A tiny hiccup of hysterical laughter welled in her throat.

He flinched and his beautifully sculpted lips quivered slightly before he replied, in a totally expressionless tone, 'They'll be saying Sam Rourke is in love with you, of course.'

Shock froze her as she searched his sardonic face. 'And will they be right?' she whispered hoarsely.

'Yes.' The mocking irony was absent from his face as he replied.

Lindy was paralysed. By the time she could speak— a small, strangled croak as it happened—the only thing left to recall Sam's presence was the draught from the slammed door.

Elated, confused, she felt like crying and laughing at the same time. How could he? she silently raged. She paced around the room, unable to sit still. How could he say *that* and then walk away? It was inhuman! It was cruel! It was so like a man! She was oblivious to the pain as she wrung her slim hands.

If the damned man loves me, why doesn't he stay around to do something about it? she thought despairingly.

She made her way to Hope's bedroom.

'Hope, are you awake?' Lindy opened the bedroom door and repeated the question.

'I am now. What's wrong?'

'I shouldn't have disturbed you.' I'm selfish, she decided guiltily as Hope blinked in the light of the lamp she'd switched on. 'I'll go...' she said half-heartedly.

'Don't be stupid. Sit down.' Hope patted the bed and sat upright.

'If I don't talk to someone I think I'll explode,' Lindy confided, taking the place her sister offered.

'Well, we can't have that—too messy. Go on, spit it out,' she advised with a resigned smile.

'I don't know whether you'd noticed, but me and Sam...Sam and I...'

'I'd noticed.'

'The thing is, I asked him if he loved me.'

Hope's eyes widened and the last vestiges of sleepiness vanished from her expression. 'You did *what*?'

'I asked him if he loved me.'

'And I always thought Anna was the outspoken one.' She looked at her sister with amazement. 'The suspense is killing me, Lindy. Are you going to tell me what he said?'

'Yes—I mean he said yes, not yes, I'm going to tell you.'

Hope seemed to have no trouble deciphering this garbled reply. 'Wow!' she whispered, her eyes shining. 'Wow!' she repeated again. 'Well, go on, tell me all!' she said impatiently.

'That is all. He didn't say anything else—he left.'

'I don't believe it!' Hope groaned. No wonder Lindy looked dazed. 'That was one exit line he'll find difficult to top. Here, have a bit of this cover,' she added anxiously. 'You're shaking like a leaf.'

'I think I'm in shock.'

'The big question is, are *you* in love?'

Palms together, Lindy pressed her fingertips to her lips. 'I told myself I could cope with an affair, but who wouldn't be in love with him? He's as close to perfect as it gets!'

This glowing commendation from her cautious sister brought a furrow of concern to Hope's smooth forehead. 'I agree he's a love, Lindy, but don't put the man on a pedestal.'

'I don't...I haven't!' Lindy responded, with a self-conscious flush. 'I've never met anyone like him before. He's nothing like I imagined.'

'All the more reason to take things slowly.'

'Is there any reason why I can't enjoy the journey?' Lindy's eyes twinkled impishly.

'None that I can think of. In fact, it's about time you had some fun, sis.'

Lindy got up from the bed. Halfway to the door she stopped and turned back. 'You know, all I ever expected of this was a sort of holiday romance. I'd convinced myself I could accept it on those terms, but now...! Everything suddenly seems very complicated. I hardly know him! There's my work and his—long-distance relationships are fraught with problems.'

She chewed her full lower lip and uncertainty flickered across her face. 'It never occurred to me I'd ever feel I should tell him about Paul and the baby.' The words came out in a rush. Over the years it was a subject none of the triplets had referred to directly.

Hope's expression sobered and her eyes were compassionate. 'That's up to you, Lindy. I thought you'd stopped feeling guilty about that. You were the victim, Lindy; it was that bastard who should have suffered!'

'Nothing is that clear-cut,' Lindy said sadly. If it was she'd be deliriously happy now, instead of being torn apart by conflicting emotions.

Of course it was true that she hadn't known Paul was

married when she'd fallen for him. It was true he'd abused his position of responsibility as her personal tutor at medical school. It was true she'd been a naive, starry-eyed teenager a long way from home, but she *had* been infatuated and she *had* thrown herself at him.

It was when she'd told him about the baby that the scales had been torn from her eyes. He'd been furious. He already, it transpired, had a family. It had got very nasty—he'd deny paternity, he'd said, if she made the mistake of telling anyone.

'It could be anyone's,' he'd sneered. 'The best thing you can do is get rid of the thing!'

The memory of the ugly words still had the power to make Lindy shudder. The humiliation and pain had been agonising.

If her sister Anna's touring dance company hadn't been in town at that moment Lindy didn't know what would have happened. As it was, it had been Anna who had taken charge. Losing the baby so early had meant that nobody other than the three sisters, not even their parents, knew about this episode.

Lindy had lived with guilt over the years, but it hadn't been the affair itself that had plagued her conscience. There had been a part of her—a small part, admittedly—that had been relieved when she'd miscarried. Her pregnancy had been short, but there had been time for her to acknowledge the growing resentment she felt for the innocent life she carried. Would she be reminded of Paul every time she looked at the baby? The face which she'd once held dear now filled her with disgust. This was something she could never forgive herself for. Every time she saw an innocent child she was freshly reminded of how, in her thoughts, she'd betrayed her own flesh and blood.

She was finding it tough; he could see that. He wanted to make it easier for her, but Sam knew Lindy was too

independent to welcome his intervention. Damage limi-
tation meant he wasn't denying or confirming any of the
mad rumours which were circulating. The crew were
watching them both like hawks. In fact they'd almost
upstaged the Dallas-Lacey debacle completely.

He cursed the fact that his lack of control in front of
the cameras meant Rosalind had been thrown into the
deep end of the circus that was his life, or a part of it
anyway. He closed his eyes momentarily and could recall precisely the rush of blind rage he'd felt when that
scummy journalist had leered at Rosalind. Sometimes,
he reflected, a man had to be hit over the head before
he could see what had been staring him in the face.

Any woman he loved would have to learn to handle
the scrutiny of cameras. There were limits to how far he
could protect his loved ones. She'd hated it yesterday;
disgust and panic had been written clear on her face, he
recalled with disquiet. Over the years could that expo-
sure drive a wedge between them? God, what was he
thinking about? He reined in his mental scenarios
abruptly. There had to be some point when you stopped
analysing and started trusting, he told himself angrily.
Stop thinking and start feeling, man!

'About the next scene.' Sam turned his attention back
to Will Gibson who stood beside him.

'Marvellous ability, that.'

'What's that, Will?'

'Thinking and falling in love. Any mere mortal would
let their work suffer, but not our lord and master. I think
everyone was expecting a holiday today after seeing you
being all brooding and masterful on the telly. Has no
one told you a man's supposed to be distracted and soul-
ful when he's in love? Nose to grindstone I can take,
but this pace is killing me—I'm not a young man!'

'Neither will I be by the time this movie's finished.'

Will grinned. He'd bet heavily against a sound technician that it was the sister Sam was interested in, and
he was feeling pretty smug, not to mention flush, just
now.

'I hear and obey. Just tell the lady to go a bit more
gently on the back next time, will you?' He chuckled
wickedly as Sam shot him a startled look. Deep colour
seeped slowly under the younger man's tan. He'd managed to embarrass Sam Rourke, which was a first, he
thought with delight. 'You wouldn't take off your shirt
for that black and white flashback, dear chap,' he explained. 'I was most put out if you recall. My lighting
would have been perfect. I know you're not a coy type
so I just put two and two together.'

'I suppose it's too much to hope I'm the only person
you've shared that little tale with?' Sam recovered his
equilibrium swiftly.

A heartless laugh was his reply.

'I want a word.'

Lindy stifled a shriek as a hand shot out to detain her.
'You've had several,' she reminded Sam tartly.

Lindy had spent a gruelling hour talking him through
a scene where he was meant to perform an emergency
tracheotomy. Her attention span had been disastrously
short—a fact Sam had shown little understanding for.
He'd made several cutting comments when she hadn't
immediately given him replies to his queries about the
procedure. The memory of these still brought a flush of
anger and mortification to her cheeks. To make matters
worse, a lot of people who wouldn't usually have bothered watching the rehearsal had suddenly developed a
great interest in the scene.

By the end of the scene Lindy had decided she must
have imagined what he'd said last night. Nobody could
be that impersonal, not to mention plain nasty, if he

loved you. And that hadn't been the only thing she'd had to contend with today. There had been the conversations that had stopped the instant she'd come within earshot and the sudden, stifled giggles.

Most of the comments had been light-hearted, but a few had been snide. Ned Stewart had given her a reproachful look that had almost made her want to apologise. She'd realised just in time that she didn't have anything to apologise for. Well, Sam's behaviour this morning ought to have dispelled any ideas some people had about preferential treatment!

'Private words; we need to talk.'

Under the impact of his brilliant blue eyes her aggression slipped silently away. 'I suppose we do.' Exhilaration and trepidation fought for supremacy.

'Meet me at my trailer at, say...' he glanced at his wristwatch '...seven-thirty.' Without waiting for her reply, he was gone.

Her feet still hadn't quite touched the ground when she bumped into Magda Gilmour from Make-Up. 'Love conquers all' wasn't a concept she'd ever placed much faith in, but Lindy was determined to give it as much help as she could. She and Sam could have something very special.

'Sorry, I didn't see you,' she apologised.

'I was looking for your sister.' Magda had one of those little-girl-lost voices that men appeared to find attractive. The appeal of the soft, high tones was lost on Lindy. This wasn't a woman she instinctively warmed to; despite the helpless air there was a hardness about the pretty face that she didn't like.

'She was looking for you the last time I saw her.'

'How annoying. I know what you're going through.'

The statement, out of the blue, captured Lindy's wandering attention. 'I beg your pardon?'

'I mean, *I've* been in the same situation as you—with Sam.'

Lindy's expression did not invite further confidences. She recalled some piece of gossip Hope had once relayed that seemed to confirm this assertion. 'That's none of my business.'

It was pretty evident that Magda hadn't stumbled across her accidentally at all. She could almost feel sympathy for the jealousy that could drive a woman to demean herself in such a way. I hope this doesn't get messy, she silently prayed.

Magda gave a sympathetic smile and patted her arm. 'You're going to need all your friends.' She saw the tiny flicker of uncertainty in the English girl's eyes and continued, in a voice that overflowed with saccharine sincerity, 'Superficially he's so warm and charming, but underneath he's totally ruthless. He uses people—especially women.'

For a split second Lindy felt trapped by her fears. Had she been blind for the second time in her life? But it only lasted for the blink of an eye, then she was seeing Sam the way she had the last few weeks. There were no murky depths to the man she knew—he was painfully open. She mentally shook herself, feeling ashamed for the moment's weakness.

'I appreciate your concern, but if I want to know anything about Sam's life I'll ask him,' she replied quietly. She deliberately kept anything which might be construed as aggression out of her voice.

She had a lot to come to terms with herself before she started worrying about a stranger's jealousy. It didn't really matter whether Magda's interest stemmed from malice or mischief because she, Lindy, wasn't interested.

The dignified confidence brought a flare of anger to the other girl's face. 'And you think he'll tell you?' She gave a scornful laugh. 'You think you know all about him, don't you? Then he must have told you about his kid?' Malicious satisfaction curved her full red lips as Lindy froze, all the colour seeping out of her skin. 'I'm not surprised. He doesn't tell many people. He wouldn't marry her, of course. He doesn't even acknowledge the boy! It's all very hush-hush—it wouldn't be good for his image at all if people found out.'

'I don't believe you.' Lindy's lips felt like ice as she forced the words out.

'Go ask him, then.'

'Quit bellyaching,' Sam advised a fellow actor. 'We're all hot and we're all tired.' He turned to a technician and said something which appeared to galvanise the small group into action.

Lindy ignored the voices that told her they were shooting and walked straight up to Sam.

'I want to talk to you.'

'Cut!' he snapped, turning to her.

Lindy's whole attention was focused on him. The fact that he was holding onto the shreds of his temper with difficulty made no impression on her. She felt no embarrassment that people were watching her and Sam, waiting for him to blow up. She didn't even hear her sister's anxious voice.

Sam looked at her face and his expression shifted from anger to concern. 'Are you ill?'

She avoided the hand he stretched out. 'No,' she denied. 'I just need to talk to you—now.' She walked away, leaving him to follow her.

'Do you want to tell me what this is all about?' Sam had only paused long enough to give instructions to the crew.

Lindy watched as he closed the trailer door. She realised for the first time that he was in costume. He was wearing a dinner jacket and black tie. He looked watch-

How To Play:

No Risk!

1. With a coin, carefully scratch off the 3 gold areas on your Lucky Carnival Wheel. By doing so you have qualified to receive everything revealed — 2 FREE books and a surprise gift — ABSOLUTELY FREE!

2. Send back this card and you'll receive brand-new Harlequin Presents® novels. These books have a cover price of $3.99 each in the U.S. and $4.50 each in Canada, but they are yours TOTALLY FREE!

3. There's no catch! You're under no obligation to buy anything. We charge nothing — ZERO — for your first shipment. And you don't have to make any minimum number of purchases — not even one!

4. The fact is thousands of readers enjoy receiving books by mail from the Harlequin Reader Service®. They enjoy the convenience of home delivery...they like getting the best new novels at discount prices, BEFORE they're available in stores...and they love their *Heart to Heart* subscriber newsletter featuring author news, horoscopes, recipes, book reviews and much more!

5. We hope that after receiving your free books you'll want to remain a subscriber. But the choice is yours — to continue or cancel, anytime at all! So why not take us up on our invitation, with no risk of any kind. You'll be glad you did.

No Cost!

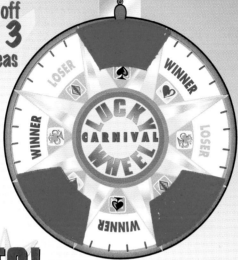

LUCKY
Find Out Instantly The Gifts You Get
Absolutely FREE!
Carnival Wheel
Scratch-off Game →

Scratch off ALL 3 Gold areas

YES!

I have scratched off the 3 Gold Areas above. Please send me the 2 FREE books and gift for which I qualify! I understand I am under no obligation to purchase any books, as explained on the back and on the opposite page.

306 HDL CY4Y   **106 HDL CY4Q**

NAME (PLEASE PRINT CLEARLY)

ADDRESS

APT.#   CITY

STATE/PROV.   ZIP/POSTAL CODE

(H-P-04/00)

BUSINESS REPLY MAIL
FIRST-CLASS MAIL   PERMIT NO. 717   BUFFALO, NY

POSTAGE WILL BE PAID BY ADDRESSEE

HARLEQUIN READER SERVICE
3010 WALDEN AVE
PO BOX 1867
BUFFALO NY 14240-9952

NO POSTAGE
NECESSARY
IF MAILED
IN THE
UNITED STATES

ful, tense, but there was a strong sense that he could explode any moment. Lindy felt strangely objective as she summed him up.

'I was talking to Magda...'

'Is that all?' He visibly relaxed. A grain of irritation even entered his voice. 'It's the last time I let sentiment overrule common sense when I employ someone. I can explain about Magda.'

Lindy made an imperative gesture and cut in impatiently, 'She told me you have a son.'

'Did she?'

His expression gave as little away as his words, but Lindy knew no denial meant only one thing. She felt physically sick. The blood was thundering in her ears. Please let him deny it, she prayed. Please!

'Do you, Sam?' Everything seemed to be happening in slow motion. Every small detail of the scene was etching itself on her consciousness.

'I was going to tell you about him when the time was right.'

'And when would that have been?' Her voice was brittle and accusing, but it was the expression in her eyes that checked his intent to touch her. She was looking at him with icy condemnation. He recoiled from the rejection he saw there.

'From your reaction, I'm not sure it would have made any difference.' The joy was suddenly gone from the day; she was a stranger. 'Ben is—'

'You know his name, then?' she cut in scornfully.

'Ben is nearly thirteen.'

'You can do simple mathematics, Sam, but how many of his birthdays have you seen?'

A flicker of something close to pain passed across his face, but Lindy was too caught up in her own orgy of anguish and disillusionment to notice. How could she have been so stupid? She'd been taken in by his charm, but it was all superficial. He was no different from Paul.

'There are circumstances which make it impossible...'

'Sure there are,' she sneered. 'There always are. Circumstances like your lack of backbone and decency. It's easy to see now why you left Ohio. You were running away from your responsibilities.' Her voice rose to a high, anguished cry of accusation.

'If you'd listen for one minute I'd tell you why I was working away from home. We were only eighteen, for God's sake.'

'We! I'm surprised you didn't conveniently forget the mother the same way you did the child!'

Pleading youth and innocence was no defence in Lindy's eyes. Being young and innocent all those years ago hadn't meant that she didn't live with the consequences. If she hadn't been so young and devastated back then perhaps she'd have been able to say these things on her own behalf, rather than for some unknown woman. The empathy she was experiencing was intense.

'I have not forgotten Ben or Marilyn.' He didn't raise his voice, but every syllable vibrated with hostility. Teeth clamped together in a savage smile, he continued, 'It's strange, but I never suspected everything was so black and white to you.' The look of distaste on his face fanned her anger to further heights.

How dared he look down his nose at her? 'When it comes to men who desert their children there can be no excuses, no grey areas to hide in. You don't even have the guts to admit what you did.'

'You really do like to take the moral high ground, don't you, Rosalind?' There was nothing covert about his contempt now. 'Well, here's one mistake I'm quite willing to admit. I thought you were a warm, sensitive woman. I just hope, for your patients' sake, that you allow a glimmer of compassion into your professional life.'

'I save my compassion for the woman and child you deserted!' she yelled back. He was turning everything around, making it sound as if *she* were the one at fault. He was totally shameless.

'I didn't desert anyone, but I don't think that's something I want to discuss with you.'

'Because I'm not the gullible little fool you took me for?'

'You're certainly not what I thought you were.'

There was an empty finality in his voice that brought home for the first time how much she'd lost. It was never there to lose, she reminded herself. I was in love with a phoney. I've found him out and he doesn't like it—they never do.

'Then it's just as well this was nothing but an on-location fling. They're nothing to write home about, are they? You told me so yourself.' Her stance defied him to deny the accuracy of her face-saving lie.

He shrugged his broad shoulders and pushed open the door, his whole attitude one of dismissal. 'I may not see my son very often,' he said, looking at her coldly, 'but at least I can be sure he's not being brought up by an intractable, self-righteous hypocrite.'

He gave a low, hard laugh. 'Was it self-righteous or hypocritical you object to?' he enquired, as a sound of inarticulate wrath escaped her lips. 'Could it be you've got a few skeletons of your own? I see you have.' He appeared to take savage pleasure from her thinly disguised distress. 'Don't worry, Doctor, I'm not interested enough to find out what they are.' The slam of the door shook the trailer.

When Hope found Lindy two hours later, walking towards her car, there were no outward signs of the tears.

She'd stopped shaking too, and she'd lost that glow which had so delighted her sister. The blank expression in Lindy's eyes made Hope want to scream with frustration. The barriers were back up with a vengeance.

'You had a fight.' It wasn't a question. 'Sam's just verbally flayed anyone stupid enough not to keep out of his way. He gave a performance that was so scary—even to me—you've probably got him an Oscar nomination. You always get the impression he's holding something back when he's performing,' she mused, falling into step beside her sister, 'but today he let us have both barrels!'

'Glad to have been of use,' Lindy said bitterly. God, these people were so self-obsessed. She'd be glad to get back to normal life.

'Ouch! I didn't mean to sound uncaring. I'm sure you two will get back together. Will is taking bets on it, and he's pretty shrewd. He rarely loses money.'

'Well, this time he's backed the wrong horse. I loathe and detest Sam Rourke and if I never see him again it'll be too soon!'

Hope recoiled at the virulence in her sister's voice. 'This isn't like you.' She held up her hands in a pacific gesture as her sister threw her a fulminating look. 'As for not seeing him again, you're working with the man for another three weeks. After that we're back to the studio and you're a free agent.'

'Oh, God!' Lindy groaned. 'I didn't really think about that. I can't do it.' She covered her trembling mouth with her hands. Work alongside him for three whole weeks? The prospect of it made her stomach tighten with dread.

'Well, if I explain to Sam how you feel, how upset you are, I'm sure he won't hold out for his pound of flesh.'

Lindy's head snapped up. 'Upset?' she repeated in an accusatory manner. 'I'm not upset, and I won't have that smarmy snake thinking I am. I'll show him I don't give that!' She snapped her fingers and tossed her head defiantly.

It would be useful, Hope mused, to be able to use this moment when she had to produce shock and amazement for the camera. I just might get an Oscar too, she thought.

CHAPTER SIX

THE caterers had taken over the entire house and gardens. Tired of the confines of her bedroom, Lindy took refuge in the smallish room that Lloyd used as his study. Lloyd was a great host and she'd lost most of her initial animosity towards him. Though she still thought he had taken advantage of her sister's friendship, that was Hope's business.

She missed the charm of the cottage in Owl Cove and the constant sound of the sea. In a short space of time the cottage had wormed its way into her heart. The less she contemplated what a pushover her heart had been lately the better! At least these plush surroundings held no memories for her, she reflected. She was determined to dwell on the positive aspects of her present predicament—such as they were.

She looked at the inevitable TV screen and struggled with the masochistic desire to turn it on. 'What the hell?' she said defiantly, and pointed the remote control at the oversized screen.

Nothing in Lloyd's house was done on a small scale. These were the sort of surroundings she'd once imagined Sam Rourke in—extravagant and ostentatious. An image of the clean, uncluttered cabin on his boat entered her head. She blinked hard to dispel the illusion that held so many painful associations for her.

'And what do you think, Sam?'

Her attention was instantly riveted to the screen. The person speaking was half a head shorter than Sam. Her silver-blonde hair was cropped short and the outrageous gold lamé dress she wore appeared to have been painted on her generous curves. Sam had to be pretty familiar with those curves, at least professionally, because Diana Hardcastle had acted opposite him in at least two films Lindy was aware of.

The sight of his tall, instantly recognisable figure made her wish she'd held out against the craving to switch on the TV. The bittersweet longings washed over her in a great tidal wave. She had the power in her hand to switch off the hateful image, she could even pretend she hadn't felt the knife-like thrust of jealousy, but she didn't—*couldn't*!

Sam was speaking now, but Lindy was aware of the sound rather than the content of his words. He had that special talent which made every person listening think he was speaking directly to them. Sam's career had begun on television and, in years gone by, he'd been the recipient of some of these awards. Tonight he was a co-presenter. A reluctant one, if Lloyd was to be believed, but getting the new film mentioned on coast-to-coast TV was worth a few sacrifices—at least that was Lloyd's view. Lindy was no longer in a position to know what Sam thought. And I care less, she thought with a spurt of defiance.

The programme proceeded pretty much to the formula of those glittery occasions, but who received the prestigious prizes was lost on Lindy. She sat, unable to tear her eyes from the screen until the last credits had rolled. Then, mentally and physically drained, she sank back into the soft leather upholstery and closed her eyes.

It was easy intellectually to dismiss Sam as a shallow, egocentric, selfish monster, but the feelings that churned in her belly didn't originate from her brain, not the sane part anyway! To be able to look at him without pretending not to, without keeping her expression blank, had been a major indulgence. She despised herself for the weakness that made her wallow in the luxury. As

tough as it was to see him most days, it was, she suspected, going to be harder when she had to go cold tur-
key in a week's time.

Wearily she ran her fingers through her fair hair; the
black ribbon that secured the ponytail slithered free, but
she made no attempt to retrieve it. What will I do? she
wondered, filled with self-derision. Allow myself two
videos a week and gradually wean myself off? In those
videos he was usually making love to other women so
that would prove a cold comfort, she thought.

I've got to pull myself together, she told herself
sternly. He has! If the gossip on set was true the divine
Diana Hardcastle, who had co-presented with him tonight, had been seen several times with him during the
past two weeks. Lindy had seen them for herself on
set—a very tactile lady, Diana Hardcastle, and Sam
hadn't appeared to mind in the least when she'd draped
herself all over him at every opportunity. No, Sam
hadn't wasted any time!

She glanced at the clock on Lloyd's desk. She'd have
to slip away back to her room soon. Like Cinderella, she
reflected, only, unlike Cinderella, she was running away
before the ball and she didn't have a ballgown either.
With a wry smile she looked down at the vanilla-
coloured silk shirt she wore tucked into the belted waist
of a pair of toffee linen trousers. The activity which had
thrown the house into chaos was for a post-award party
Lloyd was throwing. It was a good opportunity to network and push the film, he'd explained. Lloyd lived to
network! Sam would be there, Hope had warned her, and
Lindy had hated the sympathy in her eyes.

It hadn't been a lie when she'd told Lloyd, 'It's not
my sort of thing.' Hope, of course, would blend in perfectly with all the glittering, beautiful people. She'd gone
along tonight as Lloyd's partner, just to perpetuate the

deception, and she'd looked like a glorious, exotic flower in a red silk designer gown.

Lindy rotated her head to release some of the tension in her neck. I'd have hated having to be Sam's consort on occasions like this, she told herself practically. What a lucky break it was that I discovered he was a rat.

You just had to look at a situation from the right angle to see the silver lining! she reflected stoically. Sam would be far happier with a trophy girlfriend whose goals were as self-centred as his, she decided scornfully.

Sam timed his exit to make sure nobody noticed his retreat. He closed the door and the party noise became a low hum. He walked over to the bureau beside Lloyd's desk and pulled out a bottle of Scotch. He covered the bottom of a heavy crystal glass with the pale fluid and, after loosening his tie, swallowed it back in one gulp. He looked with irritation at the game show on the TV screen, but didn't bother switching it off. Couldn't be bothered just about covered his present mood.

He'd done his duty for one evening. He'd exchanged bitter words with Lloyd when he'd been presented with a *fait accompli* about tonight. Next he'll be asking me to open shopping malls and judge baby shows! he thought. He gave a short, ironic laugh. And I'll probably agree, he admitted. It was all very well to lose yourself in work. The problem was that outside work he couldn't seem to make himself give a damn about anything.

Unlike Lloyd he wasn't a natural publicist. He preferred to be involved with the creative side of things rather than marketing, which was probably why his association with Lloyd worked out so well under normal circumstances. At least something in his life was working! Sam slammed the glass down with unwanted force, a bitter, brooding expression on his face. A pile of papers slithered to the floor. With a muttered curse he bent down to pick them up. Something caught his eye—a pair of brown leather loafers, one still attached to a foot—a small narrow foot. Dropping the papers, he walked over to the leather sofa. He caught his breath sharply, even though he'd been half prepared for what he'd find there.

She lay curled up, one arm under her head, the other thrown out in an oddly defenceless gesture. One leg was tucked up underneath her, the other dangled over the edge of the seat. Her head thrashed restlessly and she gave a faint, inarticulate moan. The silk of her shirt rose rapidly, in time with her escalating respirations. The tranquil appearance of her sleeping features was disturbed by a deep frown line between her eyebrows. As he watched, her lips moved silently.

Maybe, he reflected, she can sense I'm here. My perfidy can even disrupt her sweet dreams. His lips curved in a viciously bitter smile. God help me, but I hope she doesn't have too many of those at the moment, he thought to himself. He didn't feel inclined to be generous! When the thrashing movements of her head became more violent he bent closer. She was talking—mumbling really, saying the same thing, over and over. He knelt beside the sofa and strained to catch the words which fell from her lips.

'Not the baby…not the baby…please!'

He straightened up, a frown on his face, and at the same moment Lindy shot upright, her eyes wide and filled with horror. Her piercing cry drowned out the hysterical clamour on the TV set, but didn't impinge on the noise in the other room.

Panic engulfed her and she was fighting for air. Her memory held no record of the nightmare, but the feeling of dread persisted.

'Oh, Sam,' she breathed, laying her head against the broad chest so fortuitously close. Her fingers curled into the fabric of his shirt and she trembled as his hands ran softly down the length of her back. Suddenly she stiffened. 'No!' With a sharp cry of rejection she pushed hard against him.

He caught hold of her upper arms as she jerked upright. The look on his dark face paralysed her. Stark and needy, his compulsive gaze moved over her face, before sliding lower to examine her body with the same hungry urgency.

Her mind was too numbed to try to work out how she came to be here, with her in his arms. A need just as stark and basic as his was coursing through her veins. The words of rejection never left her tongue as he took her face between his two strong hands. His thumbs moved over the downy flesh of her cheek and his eyes followed the motion. Lindy was mesmerised. His eyes met the luminous glow of hers before he moved in to touch her lips.

Softly—so softly, then his flicking tongue teased, tracing the outline of her lips, tasting the moist sweetness of her mouth. Lindy's hands stopped clutching at empty air and clutched at his shoulders.

'I can't stand this...' she moaned raggedly. Lindy was conscious of the brief flare of ferocious satisfaction in his eyes. Sam let out a deep, shuddering groan and his mouth covered hers. A kiss wasn't enough to satisfy the hunger that drove them both, even a kiss that was as all-consuming as this. Sam's fingers slipped the buttons on her shirt free as his teeth tugged at the inside of her bottom lip, her earlobe. He flicked the front-fastening catch on her bra and levered himself up on one arm to look at her. She could feel the deep shudder that rippled through his long, lean frame.

Lindy pulled him back down. She needed to feel his body against her and she delighted in the slow, erotic thrust of his hips. Her body arched frantically beneath his and her hands tugged at his clothes, impatient to be rid of the barrier between them.

Sam shrugged off his jacket. Lindy rained small, wild kisses on his face, his brown corded neck. Her fingers tangled deep in his dark, sweat-dampened hair. A series of soft pleas fell from her lips, but Sam remained silent. The wildness in his tense features gave her a moment's hesitation—there was none of the tenderness she had grown to expect in him, just blind, relentless instinct.

Her hoarse cries were drowned as his mouth fused with hers. Lindy felt as if they were sealed together and she wanted it that way. She wanted to taste him on her tongue always. She wrapped her legs around him as their movements became frenzied and frantic. The air was abruptly expelled from Sam's lungs as they rolled off the sofa and landed on the floor.

Positions reversed, Lindy looked down into his face, all sharp angles and slitted eyes—the face of a stranger. 'Are you all right?' she asked breathlessly.

She pushed back the silky strands of hair that hampered her vision. Sam's shirt had come adrift from the waistband of his trousers and several buttons were ripped off. She could see his ribcage rise and fall in time with his rapid inhalations and the concave hollow of his muscled, washboard belly. Her dazed glance registered these facts slowly.

Sam didn't reply. He caught either side of her unbuttoned shirt in each hand. The muscles in his throat worked as his eyes followed the gentle sway of her pale breasts. He pulled until the pink tips of her breasts touched the skin of his hair-roughened chest.

'I will be,' he rasped. 'I will be...'

It was the first thing he'd said to her. She ought to have objected to the complacent certainty in his words, but how could she when his words were the only thing that had made sense to her for a long time? He was right! It was the *only* way anything could be all right again.

Her weight was suspended on her hands, which rested at either side of his face. Sam captured the two narrow wrists and her weight fell full on him. His hands moved to the curve of her taut buttocks. Lindy's head fell against his shoulder as the thrust of his hips against the softness of her belly ripped a cry from her throat—it was an eerie, lost sound. Her warm breath came in short, frantic bursts against his neck. His mouth worked its way up the side of her throat, leaving the scorching marks of his hot, luscious kisses on her receptive flesh.

It was crazy and insane—one portion of her mind recognised this—but this acknowledgement was swiftly eclipsed by the age-old cry of flesh calling to flesh. This was not the time to feel embarrassed at the savagery of their coupling—that would come later!

The interruption was cruelly abrupt. Light and noise suddenly invaded the room. Sam's body prevented her from seeing the owners of the voices. Unfortunately, this didn't mean they couldn't see her. Her face flamed as she realised just *what* they were seeing. She pulled her shirt together, aware suddenly of the sensuous abandon of her posture.

'I can't imagine where he is.' Lindy could match the lilting tones to silver-blonde hair. A startled gasp sounded loud in the room.

'I rather think you've found me. If you don't mind I'm...preoccupied just now.' She felt the muscles of his upper arms bunch under her fingers, but his dry voice was totally lacking the stultifying embarrassment that everyone else appeared to be suffering from.

She felt the draught as the door was hastily closed. 'Oh, God!' Lindy's body, which had seconds earlier been molten and pliant, became rigid. She lifted her hands to her face as the first waves of humiliation hit her. How could I? she thought. In one motion she rolled onto her side and up onto her knees.

'What will they think?' she wailed.

One dark brow shot towards his hairline. 'Do you really want me to answer that?' His mood appeared to be cooling as fast as the sweat which had slickened his hot skin.

'I don't suppose you care!' she flung back angrily.

She was sick to the stomach at the ease with which he had wrecked her puny defences. Her eager capitulation made a nonsense of the iron self-control she'd fallen back on. She felt utterly and totally degraded.

'Should I?' He sat up and shrugged in an infuriatingly languid manner. 'You're making a big thing of this.'

In other words it meant nothing—less than nothing—to him. She tried not to flinch. Why give him the opportunity to gloat? She was sure that was what he wanted—that was why his blue eyes were fixed so intently on her face, so cynical and calculating.

'I don't particularly like being the butt of crude and coarse jokes.' She wrapped her hands together to make the trembling less noticeable. Her entire body was racked by intermittent tremors.

'Diana won't tell anyone what she saw,' he said confidently. 'And Lloyd isn't the type to indulge in locker-room tales. Or do you think I'm likely to boast of my conquests when I'm out with the boys?' His lip curled scornfully. 'I don't go in for that sort of male bonding.'

'It wasn't a c-conquest,' she denied. Her teeth were chattering with cold. Or was it just reaction? Her skin, which had been scaldingly hot, was now clammy and cold.

It had been Lloyd again—it seemed every time the man saw her she was ripping off Sam's clothes! If she hadn't wanted to weep she might have laughed. Sam didn't sound too bothered that his girlfriend had caught him in a very compromising situation with another woman. Why does that surprise me? she asked herself. Right at the outset his casual acceptance of marital infidelities on set should have warned her that he had warped morals. God, I was a fool to get involved in the first place, she thought, self-derision shining in her eyes. I deliberately didn't see the truth—the painful, sordid truth!

'By all means cling to the comfort of a technicality, Rosalind. I'll even resist the temptation to say "Been there, done that".' Lindy inwardly cringed at the expression of contempt on his face. 'Nobody, least of all me, is going to stop you walking around with that saintly aura of purity you like to sport.'

Her chin jerked up and her eyes flashed angrily. 'I don't!' she protested.

'No?' he drawled.

'No!' she repeated from between clenched teeth.

'Calm down; I'm not about to throw a spanner in the works. The fact you're as susceptible as the rest of us to good old-fashioned lust can be our little secret. I forgot,' he continued relentlessly. 'You like to call it *love*.' The derisive curve of his lips straightened to an unforgiving thin line. 'A pure, elevated emotion far removed from animal lust.'

Lindy snatched her shirt together as his cold gaze dwelt deliberately on the creamy swell of her breasts. He wants to hurt me! The realisation cut deeply. He was reminding her quite clearly that their primal coupling had been neither pure nor elevated! As if she needed reminding!

Sam tucked his shirt back into the waistband of his trousers. He slowly straightened his shirt, which was minus several buttons, and noticed the torn seam around one arm with elevated eyebrows. 'I forgot my needle and thread, and me a Boy Scout.'

'I doubt you ever were. Mind you, you always were prepared the way I recall it, but then I suppose your sort always takes advantage of opportunities,' she hissed.

'*My sort?* Are you trying to tell me I'd have been a better man in your eyes if I hadn't been prepared? If I'd got you pregnant?' The scathing observation made her grow pale. He couldn't possibly know that in hitting out blindly she'd managed to score an own goal with her jibe.

'I've made that mistake once,' he continued, 'and I no longer have the excuse of youth, although that's no defence in your eyes, is it, Rosalind? Actually, I don't much care for the implication that you were some sort of unwilling victim. You might have convinced yourself of that, but my memory paints a different picture.'

He seems to take a sadistic pleasure in making me squirm, she thought, forcing herself to hold his gaze— it was hard, nearly as hard as his eyes.

'Scouting is too wholesome a pursuit for anyone as depraved as me,' he went on. 'As a matter of fact, I wasn't a Boy Scout. Not because I preferred satanic rituals, though—my dad needed my help after school on the farm.'

God, but she hated the vicious sarcasm in his voice. 'How virtuous. This filial duty didn't stop you leaving home...'

'To desert my flesh and blood and selfishly sample the pleasures of the big, bad world? My, my, I can't put a thing past you, can I, darling?' The disdain in his regard made her feel petty and mean. 'Actually Dad had died by then. He sort of lost the will to go on after he lost the farm. Perhaps if Mom had still been alive...'

'I didn't know.' What could she say? She'd seen the flash of bitter loss in his eyes, though she hadn't wanted to see it. She couldn't afford empathy with this man; it was too dangerous. Yet part of her wanted to offer him comforting words. Point me to the nearest strait-jacket, she thought weakly.

'You do surprise me. Not so long ago you were very vocal about my past. I had the impression you thought you were the expert.'

'I know enough,' she said frigidly. Do I? she asked herself. For the first time she wondered if she did have enough facts. He seemed so bitter. Don't be a gullible fool, she told herself brutally. No excuse in the world could justify what he did. That was the real Sam Rourke, hard and uncompromising. He'd just been letting her see what she'd wanted to see before. Hadn't she watched him manipulate the cast and crew of the film with an expert hand? I must have been child's play! she thought.

'How do you reconcile your distaste for me with your latest performance?'

He contemplated the exact spot on the floor where...! Lindy had a vivid image of two panting bodies entwined. She placed her fingers on her temple where the blood pounded loudly. Unconsciously she shook her head in a negative gesture of denial.

'Have you decided I'll do to satisfy your more...basic needs until your perfect lover comes along?' God, why wouldn't he leave it alone? she agonised. 'The one with no skeletons in his closet? The one with no mistakes to pay for?'

'I was asleep, confused, you took advantage,' she accused hoarsely. 'I'm not looking for perfection,' she denied. The image he'd conjured up wasn't pleasant. 'I don't need a man to make my life complete—not any man!' He made it sound as if she wouldn't tolerate imperfections. That wasn't it at all, she told herself. He was twisting everything to his own purposes!

'You're making sure I pay for my mistakes, though,

aren't you?' he shot back. It was suddenly apparent that
his coolness was a façade. Underneath Sam was furiously angry. 'You could have walked out. There was
never any question of me holding you to your contract;
you knew that. But no, you have to be there every day,
Miss Sweet Serenity with a heart of stone. Even when
you're not there,' he continued in a driven voice, 'I can
smell your perfume—'

He broke off with a violent epithet. He was breathing
heavily as he raked a hand through his thick wavy hair
and glared at her. It was obvious his outburst hadn't been
intentional and he clearly regretted it.

Her head was spinning. Not for a second had she suspected he felt that way. She had been under the impression that she had been the only one going through purgatory for the past two weeks. Yet his words and his
whole attitude made it very clear the experience hadn't
been easy for him. Not by so much as a flicker had he
ever given any hint of it, she thought incredulously.

'I—I didn't know,' she faltered.

He laughed. It wasn't a pleasant sound and she
winced. 'All women know when a man wants her and I
want you.' The way he said the word made her shudder.
It was humiliating to experience an unmistakable searing
thrill of arousal in response to his low, husky statement.
Anger welled up within her and there was no external
target for it, only her own weakness.

'Oh, I don't want to,' Sam continued, unknowingly
echoing her own sentiments. 'But it seems that for the
moment I have no choice. Discovering you don't either
is a small consolation.'

'I...I don't...'

'Let's not get fatuous, Rosalind.' His incisive voice
sliced through her faltering denial. 'I've just held you in
my arms. I've felt the way your body throbbed with

need—need for me. You're as hooked as any drug addict.'

She wanted to deny it, but what was the point? She swallowed and licked her dry lips. 'I despise you.' Her voice throbbed with sincerity.

'Not as much as I do.' The self-derision in his eyes confused her even further. 'I despise myself for believing you were the first woman I'd ever met I could be myself with. I despaired of ever finding someone like that—how deliciously ironic! When I make mistakes I do it big! One day I expect you'll find that whiter-than-white guy of your dreams. Though I doubt very much he'll be able to make you feel like this...' He reached over and placed his hands around her bare midriff.

The unexpected action drove the breath from her lungs in one audible gasp. 'Let me go!'

'If I do, maybe I'll never get you out of my system,' he murmured consideringly. His splayed fingers pushed into the softness of her flesh. Not hard enough to hurt, but pain would have been preferable to the sensations the friction sent sliding deep into the pit of her stomach. He bent closer and she could smell the musky odour of his body, feel the warmth of his breath on her cheek.

'Don't be ridiculous, Sam. If you think you can scare me...' Her laugh lacked the ring of authenticity.

'I want to make love to you with my eyes open.'

He always had kept his eyes open, she recalled. He'd seemed to get pleasure from watching her. A slow flush mounted her cheeks and the heat slowly spread over her body. Sam felt it and a smile spread over his features. It didn't soften his expression, not unless hawks waiting to pounce looked soft, she reflected.

'I didn't mean that literally,' he returned, examining the hazy, half-focused expression in her eyes. 'Although that scenario has its attractions.' The rasp in his voice was a smoky invitation. 'I meant I want to make love to Rosalind Lacey, a judgemental woman with no tolerance of weakness. You're the sort of person who bandies words like "principles" and "responsibilities" a lot.' Each barb in his words burrowed deep into her skin. 'You're so smug it makes me sick. I used to think you were the medicine I needed.' His expression made it clear he'd recovered from this conviction. 'We're talking catharsis here.'

She began to struggle and Sam made no effort to restrain her. 'We!' she spat at him. 'You're the one doing all the talking.' Breathing hard, she buttoned her shirt with trembling fingers. It was temper that was making her shake, she told herself, and she had plenty of reasons to be angry!

'I can see you're the victim of my irrational behaviour.' She snorted sarcastically. 'If it's a sin to choose not to sleep with a man capable of discarding a young girl and denying his own child, I'm guilty as charged.

'Have you any idea the sort of despair she must have felt?' she asked, her voice shaking with conviction. 'She didn't have the luxury of running away. Judgemental, am I? Well, maybe I am. I do despise you because you left somebody else to suffer the consequences of your actions alone.'

'I was wrong.' His narrowed eyes held an arctic expression, and his sensual lips were thinned to a line of distaste. 'You'll never find any man who can live up to your high-minded principles, Rosalind. He doesn't exist. You don't pause for breath, do you? In you wade, judge, jury and enthusiastic executioner. No "Tell me what happened, Sam".' He saw the sudden look of confusion on her face and he threw his dark head back and laughed. It was a mirthless sound. 'It didn't occur to you, did it?'

'I'm not the one here who's done something wrong.'

'More's the pity. If, for once, you did it might make you a little less judgemental. You might be a nicer person.'

If only he knew! At least she'd discovered the truth before she'd told him. 'Don't play the wounded innocent with me, Sam. You're so clever at reversing the roles.'

'I've never pretended to be an innocent, Rosalind. I'm all for old-fashioned decency and, despite what you think, I've always tried to do the right thing by those close to me. Unlike you, I've never been all that attracted by perfection, but I do appreciate warmth, tolerance and a sense of humour. Sometimes first impressions are right—you *are* an uptight, cold bitch!'

Lindy recoiled from the full force of antipathy in his voice. 'I'd rather be that than another easy victim of your debatable charms. Even those are going to wear a little thin as the years pass by. Don't worry, though, because there'll always be plenty of young, hungry actresses ready to use you to get a few steps up the ladder. Some people might call it pathetic, but I'd say it's more of a symbiotic relationship.'

He picked up something small from the floor and, with a flick of his wrist, flung it towards her. Lindy automatically caught it. She looked at the gold engraved cuff-link in the palm of her hand.

'Keep it, as a memento.'

'Goodbye, Sam.' She curled her fingers around the cuff-link hard enough to leave the imprint on her palm.

His expression was stony as she slipped out through the French windows. That goodbye had had a ring of finality to it and he knew for certain that he'd need a new medical advisor for the last week of filming. Nostrils flared, breathing hard and fast, he told himself that that suited him just fine!

Lindy ran up the metal spiral staircase that led from the veranda to her bedroom. She ran to the wardrobe and pulled out her suitcase. Pausing only to blot the tears from her cheeks, she began to fling her clothes into the case. She swept the dressing table clear of her personal items and threw them on top. With a determined expression on her face she closed the lid.

She'd had enough of actors and parties and boring, boring days on set. No wonder they paid actors well; something had to compensate for the tedium. Most of all she'd had enough of Sam Rourke! With that thought in mind she began to cry in earnest.

CHAPTER SEVEN

THEY were about to pay for the lengthy Indian summer.
There were a few ominous rumbles in the distance. The
dry ground was suddenly struck by a deluge as the rain
began. The dark figure sitting in an anonymous black
car turned on the windscreen-wipers and waited.

An ambulance with flashing lights pulled up in front
of the wide doors of the casualty department, but his
attention didn't stray from the swing-doors. It was hot
and sultry, and his shirt clung damply to his back. When
he'd requested a car which would blend in he hadn't
anticipated no air-conditioning. When he'd complained,
Hope had laughingly told him that roughing it would do
him good.

He'd been sitting there for two hours and had been
eyed suspiciously by the grey-uniformed security guard
before the figure he'd been waiting for appeared. He
watched as she stood under the canopy and peered out
at the rain. An extra-violent clap of thunder made her
take an involuntary step backwards.

He took in every aspect of her appearance at a glance,
his eyes greedily absorbing each minute detail. When
the thin cotton pinafore she wore over a short-sleeved
white cotton tee shirt billowed in the blustery wind, he
could see the faint outline of her legs. A hank of shining
soft hair slithered from the hairgrips which had dragged
it back and, as he watched, she dropped her bag and
used both hands to tuck the strands behind her ears.

Sam Rourke was not a person associated with inde-
cisiveness, but he did hesitate. Inner conflict was evident
in the drawn lines of his face. Then, with a determined

shake of his head, he pushed open the door. He had
every right to demand an explanation for her behaviour.
Face it, man, you've been well and truly duped, he said
to himself. If her spiteful vindictiveness had only affected him he might have forgiven her, but as it was...
Face grim, he closed the door and turned his attention
once more to the solitary figure—only she wasn't solitary any more. A man, tall and fair, dressed in a light-
weight suit, had emerged from the building. He was
laughing at Lindy's attempts to tame her hair and his
profile would have done justice to your average Greek
god.

His whole attitude as he bent his head was one of
familiarity—intimacy. He picked up Lindy's bag and
tucked it under one arm, the other curled around her
shoulders. Together they ran out into the rain. The car
they got into was a silver Mercedes.

The expressions that flickered across Sam's face coa-
lesced into stone as he stood there, the rain streaming
down his face. Slowly, almost as if he'd forgotten how
to accomplish the familiar task, he got back into the car.
He drove out of the car park, out of the market town
and onto the open country road. After several miles he
pulled off the road into a lay-by. Arms across the steer-
ing wheel, he laid his head on his hands. When he
straightened up again his eyes were bleak, and his manner totally composed.

The farmhouse kitchen was filled with light and warmth
on even the dullest of days. Two small figures flung
themselves at her brother-in-law and attached themselves
firmly to his long legs.

'Bess has had kittens—come see!'

'Five, we counted,' an identical voice added. 'Come
see.' They fairly danced with impatience as they released him.

'Where is this miracle of procreation?' Adam asked, giving Lindy a resigned grin.

'Your sock drawer, Uncle Adam.'

'My what?'

'You can't move her—Aunty Anna says so. She says it's your fault for leaving it open.'

'She would.'

Lindy laughed as she watched him being led off by his twin nephews.

'Aunty Hope is here too.'

This belated piece of information drifted towards Lindy. With a surge of pleasure she rushed towards the drawing room.

'Hope! Why didn't you tell me you were coming?'

'My little surprise.' Hope looked up, a quizzical smile on her face. She was seated beside the third Lacey sister. Small, slight and dark, Anna, the married triplet, managed to give an impression of vitality even when curled up amongst the cushions.

'I didn't know either,' she confirmed. 'The royal visitation took me completely unawares.'

'Less cheek, you,' Hope remonstrated.

'Come and sit down—you look whacked,' Anna observed. She pushed several cushions onto the floor and patted the space beside her.

Lindy didn't need a second invitation. The high-ceilinged room was filled with rich, earthy colours, lovely fabrics and textures, and a log fire crackled in the hearth. It was a deeply relaxing room with a warm, soothing ambience. It was a place she associated with laughter and love. There was a shadow of envy in her eyes as she looked at her glowing sister. Anna seemed to be very relaxed about her multiple pregnancy.

'I think the hours they expect you to work are ridiculous,' Anna observed. 'It's inhuman, I told Adam. I can't imagine why anyone would want to work in a casualty department.' She took a bite out of a piece of Turkish delight and gave a sigh. 'I always hated this stuff.'

'I enjoy work, and I doubt it's harder than looking after the twins twenty-four hours a day.' Lindy liked exhaustion—she needed exhaustion! Sometimes she thought the locum job in the casualty department at St Jude's, where her brother-in-law was a consultant surgeon, had saved her sanity. She had moved back home to her parents' farm and she was a frequent visitor at Anna's rambling home. It *should* have been impossible to feel lonely whilst surrounded by her loving family. Yet for some reason her sense of isolation increased daily.

'What have you done with Adam, Lindy?' Hope asked, looking around as if she expected to see him materialise.

'On the twins' list of priorities you come way down below the new kittens. Am I right?' Anna asked Lindy.

Lindy nodded. 'They hijacked him.'

Anna had taken on her husband's twin four-year-old nephews when they had married, along with a teenage niece and an older boy who was now twenty. To top that she was now expecting twins of her own, and showed every indication of thriving on what would have exhausted a lesser mortal.

'Are you staying long?' Lindy asked Hope, stroking the ears of the dog that had placed its head in her lap.

'Flying visit,' Hope said. 'I spent the morning with Mum and Dad. It's a hive of activity at the farm. Mum's been wildly baking for a WI thing at the farm tonight.'

'Why do you think I'm here? You need psychological counselling before you can take an evening of those ladies.' They took a great interest in all things romantic, and Lindy didn't feel up to a grilling, even a good-natured one.

'Talking of emotional states...?' Hope let the question hang in the air.

'If I ever meet this Sam Rourke I'll give him a piece of my mind,' Anna said grimly. 'Push that dog down, Lindy, she knows she's not allowed on the furniture.'

'Since when?' Some rules were flexible in her sister's house. The brindled mongrel gave her a melting look as she nestled more comfortably on her lap. Lindy had told Anna part, if not all, of the story. What choice did she have? Hope would have if she hadn't. At least there was very little likelihood of the scenario Anna had mentioned coming to pass.

'Actually, Anna, you might get the opportunity.' Hope had both her sisters' undivided attention. 'I came over with Sam. We're here to plug the film. We recorded the programme last night and it's going out over the weekend. When I said the visit was flying, I meant it literally. We're due in Paris tomorrow. He's picking me up later.'

Lindy had stopped listening; her sister's travel arrangements held little interest. She got to her feet, tipping the dog unceremoniously onto the floor. The animal regarded her reproachfully and flopped out in front of the log fire.

'I'm going home,' she said in an agitated voice. 'I can't be here...' Panic raced through her veins. The very idea of seeing Sam made her stomach muscles go into spasm. 'How could you, Hope?' She drew a deep, shuddering breath and glared at her sister.

'It wasn't intentional.' This much was true, but when she'd realised Lindy would be here she hadn't altered the arrangement. Part of her had hoped that they would both have come to their senses by now. She realised that she'd badly miscalculated. 'What the hell did he do to you, Lindy?'

'That's what I'd like to know,' Anna said, getting to her feet.

'What would you like to know?' Her husband had replaced his suit with cream chinos and an open-necked shirt. 'Hi, Hope,' he said casually. He coped with the presence of an international supermodel on his sofa without a flicker of surprise. He wasn't as casual as he kissed his wife. 'I hope you haven't done anything stupid today.' He lovingly patted the bulge under her baggy shirt. 'I caught this woman heaving around packing cases in the attic yesterday.'

'Don't fuss, Adam. It's the nesting instinct.'

'It's insanity,' he corrected her firmly.

'Sam Rourke is coming here,' she told her husband dramatically.

It became clear to Lindy that Anna had, predictably, shared what information she had with her husband. The menace on his face spoke volumes. 'Is he indeed?'

'Take that look off your face, Adam Deacon! I can't cope with macho posturing just now.'

After the initial shock, Adam looked more interested than offended by this sharp reprimand. This wasn't the Lindy he knew speaking.

'I don't need you, or Anna, or anyone else to protect my honour. Sam Rourke means nothing to me except an embarrassing memory.'

'If you say so.' It was Anna who replied. She kept the scepticism from her tone with difficulty. The memory of her sister arriving home six weeks ago looking like a victim of shell-shock was still fresh.

'I do.'

'In that case there's no need for you to run away, is there? Stay for supper as we planned.'

Lindy regarded Anna with dislike. Refuse and she instantly negated her previous claim, and Anna knew it. 'If you like.' She rose to the unspoken challenge and gave a casual shrug.

She was glad nobody knew how hard it was for her

to look unconcerned. Inside she was screaming, but she wasn't going to disgrace herself and start gibbering like the idiot she was. How could you love someone who had proved himself rotten to the core? she wondered bleakly. What was wrong with her? She'd lost her sanity over a pretty face—he was a chameleon, all things to all people, but underneath there was no substance. The sound of Adam's pager stopped her bitter reflections.

He picked up the phone. 'Deacon here.' He nodded several times, glanced at his watch and said, 'Fifteen minutes,' before replacing the receiver.

'I take it there's one less for supper?' his wife observed philosophically.

'A bad RTA's just come into Casualty. At least four orthopaedic consults, so it's likely I'll be in Theatre until—well, it could be any time.' He bent and kissed Hope's cheek. 'Sorry to run out on you.' He smiled at Lindy with a quizzical expression in his green eyes. 'Macho posturing,' he said admiringly. 'I expect you were taking notes, love?' he murmured to his wife.

Anna linked her arm with his. 'I don't recycle old material,' she chuckled warmly as they left the room.

'Has Sam asked...asked about me?' Lindy bit her lip and wished the words unsaid. She darted an embarrassed look at Hope's face.

'Oh, Sam's hardly had time to say more than two words to me. He's hitting every nightspot, and I'm not just talking local here; the man's been crossing time zones to party. Even Lloyd is worried about overexposure,' she reflected drily. 'When he's not partying he takes off on that boat of his. I'm an eight-hours-a-night girl myself, but I suppose you can fit more in if you cut out sleep altogether.'

'Are you trying to imply this has something to do with me?' She knew Sam would have got her out of his system long ago. She'd replayed his parting shots often enough in her head—'uptight, cold bitch', he'd called her. No, he was probably just reverting to type. It was a source of constant irritation that Hope considered him one of the good guys. Part of her longed to disillusion her sister, but that would mean raking up old memories of her own.

'I'd say he's a man who doesn't want to sit still long enough to think. Tell me, Lindy, how are *you* sleeping?' Hope asked slyly.

'Such subtlety, Hope.'

'You were so good together.'

Lindy gritted her teeth. She could do without having her sister's romantic instincts to contend with. 'If you want romance, Hope, go and find your own. I promise you it's not so rosy when you're experiencing it first-hand.'

'In my experience,' Anna commented from the door, 'it's worth hanging in there.'

'Give me strength,' Lindy breathed. 'I'm surrounded.'

'We only want you to be happy,' Hope said softly.

'You're mad if you think Sam Rourke is part of that equation!'

'What *did* he do to you?' Anna found it disorientating to see this depth of emotion on her sister's normally composed features.

Lindy felt cornered by their persistence and good intentions. 'Nothing to *me*.'

'Then what...who...?' Hope persisted.

'He has a son.' The words burst out. 'That doesn't get mentioned in the press releases, does it?' she went on bitterly. 'Or the fact he doesn't acknowledge the child, or that he deserted the teenage mother. The irony is delicious, isn't it?' she went on in an unsteady voice. 'I do seem to fall for a *very* particular type, don't I?' She didn't seem to be aware of the admission she'd just made, but her sisters exchanged knowing glances.

'Who told you this?' Hope asked.

The scepticism in her sister's voice made Lindy round on her furiously. 'Does that matter?' she accused. 'He didn't deny it!'

'But he must have given you some explanation,' Anna reasoned, lowering her enlarged frame into an armchair.

'Explanation!' Lindy yelled, looking at her as if she were mad. 'What reason could justify what he did?'

'I think you're too obsessed by your own personal tragedy to be objective or even reasonable about this, Lindy,' Anna replied. 'You can't let the past haunt you, and you shouldn't confuse every man with Paul.'

Lindy flinched. She felt betrayed by her sisters' attitude. Why didn't they just condemn him out of hand? Like you did, a voice in the back of her mind added. Why did they reserve judgement? How could they question her opinion? Didn't she have enough justification to compare Sam with Paul? The angry questions followed in quick succession through her brain.

They didn't stop her when she walked angrily from the room. The rain had become a drizzle as Lindy wandered amongst the sweet-smelling herbs of the old-fashioned kitchen garden. She crushed a stem of thyme between her fingers and breathed in the distinctive pungent fragrance.

She wasn't capable of holding onto anger for long. Eventually she cooled down enough to think rationally about her sisters' reactions. She was objective enough to accept that her reaction to Sam's past sins had been exaggerated by her personal experience. That didn't make her response any less valid, though, did it? In fact, she could appreciate better than most just how badly he'd behaved.

Did a man like that ever change, deep down? She doubted it. Should she have listened to his version of events? The thought nagged away at her until she was forced to admit she had been afraid to hear him out. Afraid that in her desperation to be with him she would accept and cling to his excuses, no matter how feeble they were. Women did it all the time—made compromises just to keep the man they loved. She was desperately afraid that she was that sort of woman. But some prices were too high to pay—even for love! She touched the breast pocket of her shirt and felt the outline of a gold stud. She kept it to remind herself how cruel he could be—at least that was what she told herself!

'Aunty Lindy, Aunty Lindy, do you want to see our worms?'

Lindy blinked away the tears from her eyes.

'We've got twenty-five.'

'We did have twenty-seven, but a bird got one and we put one under Kate's pillow, and she killed it.'

'Girls are stupid.' They spoke together with a good deal of feeling.

'I'm a girl.'

'You're a lady,' they contradicted her with impeccable logic.

'Then how can I refuse an offer like that?' Lindy took the two muddy hands in hers and was led away.

Two pairs of red wellingtons preceded the twins into the kitchen. A ginger cat with half a tail missing took the wise precaution of removing itself to the top of a pine dresser.

Anna picked up the boots with a sigh. 'If you ever want any furniture fashionably distressed, don't bother paying, just leave the item here for a couple of weeks. It's an entirely natural process.'

'I'm hungry.'

'So am I. Who are you?'

'Sam Rourke. Who are you?'

'I'm Sam too and he's Nathan. This is Aunty Lindy.'

'I know who this is. Hello, Rosalind.'

The breath literally froze in her throat. 'Sam, how are you?' Casual acquaintances said things like this, didn't they? Her hands felt numb as if they didn't belong to her and her head was extraordinarily light. I will not faint, I will not faint... The black dots that danced before her eyes receded slightly, but the rushing sound in her ears persisted.

'Is that a professional enquiry, Rosalind?'

The sound of her name on his tongue brought back a rush of memories. It was ludicrous that a word on his lips could arouse her more than any other man's love-making, but she couldn't deny the power of his voice.

He did look tired and, always lean, he looked to have lost more weight; it emphasised the mean, hungry look. The cynicism in his spectacular eyes seemed more pronounced and the planes of his face more angular. He looked a dangerous proposition, but then he always had been. She had just been blind to the fact.

The light reply wouldn't come. It congealed in her throat. Her eyes watered with the effort to tear her eyes from his face and beads of sweat broke out over her upper lip. The desire to walk straight into his arms was terrifying, especially since they weren't held open for her any more—and never would be if the cold lack of interest in his eyes was anything to go by.

'Won't you stay for supper?' Anna kindly stepped into the breach.

'No!' The word was horror-filled. Lindy closed her eyes and turned her attention to the twins, who, oblivious to the tension in the room, were playing around her feet. 'I'm sure Mr Rourke's too busy.'

Sam regarded Lindy's down-bent head for an instant. He wanted to punish her and here was a small opportunity. 'Mr Rourke would love to stay.'

'See what happens when I'm polite?' Anna said ruefully.

Sam regarded the slim brunette—slim if you discounted the swollen belly—with surprise. Neither of her sisters seemed amazed that she hadn't censored the words that had sprung to her lips.

'Kind people call Anna forthright,' Hope told him. 'Her husband calls her—'

'Not in front of the children,' Anna interrupted smoothly.

'Uncle Adam's coarse and vulgar,' a youthful voice commented, proving that children had very acute hearing.

'I like him that way,' Anna observed, by way of apology.

Sam looked disconcerted, but a shade of amusement thawed the iciness of his expression and Anna began to see what her sister might have found attractive about him—beyond the obvious.

'Can we show Sam the kittens?'

'No!' a chorus of three adult voices replied.

'If it's an inconvenience...' Sam began.

'Don't be silly. It's not every day we have a film star to dinner. Hope hardly counts, you see. I must ask you one favour,' Anna admitted. 'An autograph, for the twins' sister, Kate. She's got you plastered all over her bedroom wall. She's doing her Duke of Edinburgh expedition at the moment somewhere in Snowdonia. She'll be devastated she wasn't here. Take him through to the sitting room, Lindy. Hope can help me with the food.'

Lindy glared at her sister, who smiled cheerfully back. 'This way.' She jerked her head in Sam's direction. She wished Adam were there. Surely he wouldn't have been as unfeeling as her sisters? He, at least, would have been immune to the charisma this man exuded.

'So this is the warmth of British hospitality I've heard

so much about. Lovely room, nice quirky touches.' Sam picked up a piece of bleached driftwood that lay on a polished oak chest.

'Anna's quirky.'

'I noticed. Sexy lady.'

Lindy gasped as a stab of jealousy struck her. 'She's pregnant.' Had anyone ever looked at her and thought, Sexy lady? No, of course they hadn't—*she* was the uptight, cold bitch. Self-pity welled up inside her. Lindy knew there was nothing overt about her sexuality and she wanted it that way. She couldn't function if she imagined men were looking at her and thinking... A self-conscious flush mounted her cheeks. There had been a time when she'd liked the idea of Sam looking at her and thinking...

'I noticed that too.' Sam sat down amongst the tumbled cushions of the large sofa. 'Do I make you uncomfortable?'

You'd like that, wouldn't you? she thought, roused from her uncomfortable moment of introspection. 'It's never entirely comfortable to be reminded of your mistakes.' He hadn't liked that. The flicker of anger had been brief, but she'd seen it.

'You're working?'

'Yes, I am.'

'I'm surprised your employers didn't apply to me for a character reference, in my capacity as your previous employer. I'd have been quite happy to tell them all I could.'

'Sorry to deprive you, but Adam, my brother-in-law, is conversant with my medical skills.'

'And is his knowledge limited to that?'

'What exactly is that supposed to mean?'

'Casual curiosity.'

'It sounded like snide innuendo to me.'

'You'd know all about that.' For the first time his

feelings were not hidden behind the wall of cold indifference. What she saw made her recoil. His anger was focused and intense and she was the focus!

'I don't know what you're talking about.'

He snorted scornfully. 'Sure you don't,' he drawled. 'The same way you've no idea who told that journalist about Ben.'

'Ben?' The confused incomprehension on her face appeared to inflame him further.

'Yes, Ben, my son,' he ground out. 'Surely you didn't think I wouldn't realise it was you? How many pieces of silver did you hold out for, Rosalind?'

Lindy was trying desperately to slot the pieces of a puzzle into place. Her head hurt with the effort to concentrate her spinning thoughts. 'People know about your son?' The line between her brows deepened.

'Not yet, but they will. And you're so surprised, aren't you?' he sneered. 'If my information is reliable, the revelations are going to coincide with the release of the film.'

'You think I...?' she said in a strangled voice. Shock swept through her as she realised fully what he was suggesting.

'Show Hope your outraged innocence. I'm sure she could use it—professionally speaking, that is.'

'Sam, I didn't...'

'Don't!' He was on his feet, every inch of his body vibrating with suppressed fury. He dragged his hand heavily through his hair. 'Just don't. Don't make it worse by denying it. God, how can I have been this wrong?' Self-disgust twisted his lips into an ugly grimace. 'Look me in the eye and tell me that it wasn't you.' He looked torn—part of him willing her to do so, the other half daring her to.

No matter how things stood between them she didn't want him going away thinking she was capable of doing such a petty, spiteful thing. It hurt her that he thought she was capable of it.

'Sam, I've never...' She could at least staunch the flow of acid recriminations. Then suddenly she recalled the explanation her sisters had wrung from her earlier. Dismay clouded her eyes, the heavy thump of her heart echoed her misery.

'At least you can't lie to me.' For a moment Sam felt overwhelmed by mindless fatigue. Part of him had hoped...

Lindy closed her eyes and prayed for inspiration. What was the point in defending herself when he distorted everything she said? 'You've already made up your mind,' she accused shakily.

'Is that a privilege you reserve for yourself?' He removed his gaze abruptly from her pale face and stared at his white-knuckled hands, which clearly betrayed the violence of his feelings. He thrust them into his trouser pockets. His eyes raked her face briefly before he deliberately turned his back on her and began to pace the room.

The justice of his observation hit her painfully. It was true she hadn't given him an opportunity to defend himself. If I was as wrong as he is now... The thought made her feel physically sick. What have I done? she wondered desperately.

'Sam, you must listen,' she pleaded urgently. All she could read in his rigid shoulders was rejection. She placed a hand on his back.

Her hands sliding under his shirt—arms curled around his middle—pressing her breasts against his back... The images slipped into his head in the time it took to blink. The effort to halt this fantasy made the sinews in his neck stand out.

Sam turned as if she'd struck him. The revulsion in

his expression brought her hand to her lips to stifle a cry.

'No, *you* listen. Didn't you give any thought to the consequences of your actions?' Her silence seemed to compound his condemnation. 'Did you really think I kept silent about my son out of choice? Don't you think I'd have loved to have boasted to everyone when he learnt to ride his bike, when his team won little league?'

'I don't understand.'

'You didn't want to,' he reminded her grimly. He read the guilt in her face and his eyes narrowed. 'Marilyn was pregnant when we were both eighteen. Eighteen— God,' he half groaned. 'We were young, but not stupid enough to think we had enough going for us to sustain a marriage. I helped out financially as much as I could in the early years and her mother looked after the baby while Marilyn finished school. I saw Ben whenever possible.'

Lindy didn't think he was aware that he had forgotten for a split second to mask his vulnerability.

'Marilyn married seven years ago. He's a good man, a better father than I have ever been.' The raw despair in his voice made Lindy want to hug him. 'I could see their point of view. I'd breeze in every so often and shower the kid with gifts, but I wasn't involved in all the nitty-gritty parts of parenting. He was confused; he had two fathers, although he was too young at the time to realise that. I'd made a name for myself by then and Marilyn lived in dread of finding the media camped on her doorstep. She's not the sort of lady who would enjoy being a human-interest story.'

'You gave him up to protect him?' What have I done? Horror-struck, she could only stare at him.

'I didn't want to. I worked myself up into a frenzy of self-righteous anger the first time they suggested it. Then I sat down and faced a few cold, hard facts. I wasn't thinking about Ben; my motives were purely selfish. I haven't lost contact with him completely. Marilyn still keeps me up to date with his progress. I get photos and school reports…'

Lindy swallowed the lump of emotion in her throat. There was a bleakness in his emotionless description that touched her deeply. 'I'm so sorry, Sam.'

His head whipped round. 'Sorry!' he snarled. 'It's a bit late for that, isn't it?'

Lindy felt so miserable it hardly mattered to her that he'd assumed her apology was an admission of guilt. She *was* guilty, just not of what he thought. She was guilty of not trusting him. It would have been easier to find release in anger, but she had little room to criticise after the way she'd behaved.

'Is it in the papers yet?'

'Why? Eager to read what your poisonous seeds have sprouted? I've told you, they're only holding off to get maximum effect when *The Legacy* is released. A child's going to suffer just to satisfy your vindictive spite.'

'You can't believe I'd want that.'

'I think you wanted to hit back at me and you did the first and most vicious thing you could think of. Try telling Ben it's not personal when he gets crucified at school. Try telling the family you've just torn apart that you didn't mean it.'

'I can't be the only person who knows,' she said desperately.

'You're the only one I don't trust.'

Her head went back as if he'd struck her. Sam wanted to respond to the stricken expression in her eyes. Wanting to comfort the woman who had wrought havoc in his life was the latest in a long line of crazy things he'd done since he'd first laid eyes on Rosalind Lacey. She suckered you—when is it finally going to sink in? he asked himself.

'I don't blame you for feeling that way.' She faced him with unconscious dignity.

'That's mighty generous of you.'

'There are some things you should know.' In his present vengeful mood, telling him about Paul and the baby was probably not the wisest thing to do, but she owed him that much. 'They might help you understand why I overreacted to the things Magda told me.' Magda! She recalled the gloating spite in the other woman's voice as she'd relayed her tale. 'Have you thought about whether it could have been Magda?' she began eagerly. It had to be; it fitted.

'Don't try to worm out of it now, Rosalind. Magda's known about Ben for over a year. Why would she choose this moment to go public?'

A woman scorned, she wanted to say, but he wouldn't have heard her. He and Hope were two of the most physically blessed people she'd ever met and both had an amazing lack of vanity. He was so used to women lusting after him, he probably didn't notice one more or less.

She closed her eyes. Where do I begin? she thought. 'I've done some things I regret...'

'If you feel the urge to confess, go see a priest,' he advised harshly. 'I'm not here to make you feel better.'

'Oh, Sam!' She bit her lip and his eyes became riveted on a single scarlet droplet of blood that trembled on the pale pink fullness. 'Isn't there something you can do to stop the story?'

'You overestimate my powers. Once the machinery of the free press starts moving it flattens everything in its way.' She dabbed the spot of blood with her tongue and a shudder racked his body. 'Tell me, Rosalind, do you wreck all your boyfriends' lives or am I getting special treatment? Should I warn your blond Adonis?'

She looked at him blankly. 'I don't...'

'I saw you outside the hospital. I wanted to catch you alone, but then lover boy showed up. Silver Mercedes,' he added, with a cynical smile. 'He must have brought you home.'

God, he thought Adam... 'He's not my boyfriend; he's married.'

'From the way he was all over you that could soon change.' Sam could almost see the neon arrow over his head inscribed with the word 'jealous'. He read compassion in her eyes and wanted to break something—he didn't need Rosalind Lacey's pity!

'I've popped the boys in the bath. Would you be an angel and keep an eye on them for me, Lindy?' Anna breezed into the room.

'Yes, of course.' Lindy seized on the opportunity to escape. She didn't want to let Anna see how upset she was or she'd begin to ask some very awkward questions. Subtlety wasn't her sister's strongest point.

She was halfway up the broad, curving sweep of stairs when Sam's long legs caught up with her. 'Your sister suggested I keep you company.'

'She would!' Being an only child had distinct advantages, she reflected. 'You could have refused.'

'It would have taken a braver man than me.'

'Sometimes I don't know how Adam puts up with her!' Lindy pushed open the twins' bedroom door and picked her way over the clutter of toys.

'Is their marriage in trouble?'

Lindy gave a laugh. 'They're still at the honeymoon stage; maybe they always will be. I think they fell in love the first moment they met.' She paused to pick up a large red truck that blocked her way. 'It's not exactly a tranquil relationship. It wouldn't suit me, but they seem to like it that way. Boys, stop that!' The bathroom floor was swimming with water.

Kneeling beside the bath, Lindy returned half the plas-

tic bathroom toys to the tub. 'Try to keep some of the
water *inside* the bath, please.'

She got up, the steamy atmosphere already turning the
fine wisps of hair around her face into a halo of curls.
'You don't have to stay. I won't tell Anna.'

'I saw Ben in the bath, once.' The depth of longing
in his voice made startled tears stand out in her eyes.

He tore his eyes away from the children and looked
at Lindy.

'Don't you mind giving all this up for your married
stud? Domesticity, children,' he elaborated harshly.

Lindy knew he resented the fact that she'd witnessed
his expression of loss. 'I have my career.' She didn't
bother correcting his assumption that Adam was her
lover. While he thought that, he couldn't know how in-
complete her life felt without him. He couldn't know
she still loved him. I love him and he actually hates me,
she thought.

'Is that enough?'

'It is for you. Do you think my biological clock makes
me so different?'

'Were you always so slick at avoiding giving a
straight answer? You must be pretty crazy over this guy,
Rosalind.'

'Why?' She pulled the plug on the boys. 'Time up;
the water's getting cold.' She held open one fluffy bath
sheet and wrapped it firmly around the first body to
clamber from the bath. Rather to her surprise, Sam did
the same for his namesake. 'Get in your pyjamas before
you clean your teeth,' she instructed as they both
emerged from their vigorous rubs dry and glowing.

Sam took hold of the opposite corners of the bath
sheet she held and they folded it corner to corner. They
both took a step forward to finish the job. Sam pressed
his end of the towelling square in her hands, but didn't
quite release his grip.

'Because you are willing to forget all your high-minded principles for him,' he said, continuing their conversation as if there had been no interruption.

'I didn't say it was serious.' It occurred to her that it was faintly bizarre to conduct a conversation about a situation that didn't exist beyond Sam's fertile imagination.

'Not serious! You were ready to pillory me over a youthful indiscretion. You gave a very forcible imitation of the moral majority back then. I didn't even rate a fair hearing, and here you are sounding *casual* about sleeping with a married man! I've met some screwed-up females in my life, but you're in a class of your own!'

His fingertips brushed against the inside of her wrist and suddenly pain at his scathing comments took second place to the flood of sensation that spread from that tiny point of contact to bathe her body in a tingling glow. The desire that writhed in her belly was a dark, hungry thing that robbed her mind of rational thought in the space of a heartbeat.

'Please, Sam!' she pleaded huskily. Eyes half closed, she swayed. His hands moved up her arms, gripping the flesh of her upper arms.

He was going to kiss her—she could almost taste him. She could smell his warm body, the distinctive musky male odour that her senses had been starved of.

'What the hell are you doing?'

She was pushed away and the normal world rushed in. The world that held the noisy sounds of children in the adjoining room, the damp material twisted in her fingers and the look of disgust in the eyes of the man in front of her.

The sense of vulnerability was overwhelming. She couldn't trust herself to be in his company. 'Just do one thing for me.' She couldn't shrug off this incident with a few flippant comments or seek refuge in any more stupid deceptions. 'Please don't stay for supper.' I can't bear it, she wanted to sob. If he didn't leave soon, she probably would! I *begged* him! she thought, silently squirming with mortification.

His gaze ran slowly over her face. He reached in his pocket and pulled out a silent mobile phone. 'I just received a very urgent message.'

She sagged with relief. 'Thank you.'

'I'm not doing this for your benefit,' he said sardonically. 'I value my sanity.'

CHAPTER EIGHT

'HAVE you seen what it says in the paper today?' Beth Lacey folded the newspaper and refilled her husband's teacup.

Like most farmers, Charlie Lacey had already been up for several hours. He sat in his work clothes whilst his wife and daughter were still in their dressing gowns.

'After what they wrote about Hope I'd have thought you'd take everything you read there with a pinch of salt,' he observed, spreading jam thickly on his toast.

'Poor Hope,' Beth said.

'Poor Hope nothing; it's us that has to put up with the spiteful tongues.' Charlie Lacey still resented the slights his wife had had to contend with in the small community since the story about their daughter's fictitious affair had been splashed over the national papers.

'We know the truth, dear.' Beth received an unimpressed grunt by way of reply. 'You know him, don't you, Lindy?'

'Who?' Lindy asked lethargically.

'What time did you finish work last night?' her father demanded, shifting his attention from his food to his pale-faced daughter.

'Eleven-thirty.'

'You were out before me yesterday morning.'

'It was a split shift, Dad. I had a couple of hours free in the afternoon.'

'Couple of hours,' he snorted disparagingly. 'You should still be in bed. You look awful.'

'Thanks for sharing that,' Lindy replied drily. As much as she appreciated her parents' concern, living at

141

home after so many years' independence did have its disadvantages. 'Who is it I know, Mum?' she asked, changing the subject.

'That Sam Rourke—he's splashed all over the front cover.' There was a rustle of paper as she passed the daily to her daughter.

Lindy stared at the grainy photo with unfocused horror. So it had finally happened. Being prepared didn't lessen the sick feeling in the pit of her stomach. Even though none of Sam's accusations was true, in some strange way she did feel responsible. She couldn't bring herself to read the lurid headlines.

'So tragic,' her mother continued, oblivious to her daughter's feelings on the subject. 'That poor little boy.' She gave a sigh. 'They don't know if he'll live. What a waste.'

'What? What did you say?' Lindy said in the strangest voice her mother had ever heard.

'Why, what's wrong, dear?' Beth watched in amazement as her daughter wrestled with the paper, trying to turn the crumpled leaves to the appropriate page.

'Never mind about that! What does it say? Who won't live?' She was almost sobbing with frustration as she tried to find the front page.

'Don't use that tone with your mother.' A glance from his wife stilled Charlie Lacey's objections.

'Sam Rourke's son has been in a terrible car crash.'

The paper fell from Lindy's nerveless grasp. 'Sam's not dying?' she said in an empty voice. 'He's not dead?' she repeated carefully. She gave a sudden dry sob and pressed her fist against her lips.

'No, dear, it's his son who's critical. Mr Rourke has rushed to his side, apparently, though why that should surprise anyone I don't know. It's what parents do,' she added with a gentle smile.

'I must get dressed,' Lindy said, glancing down at her

towelling robe with an abstracted expression. 'What time is it?'

'What are you doing?' Charlie asked before his daughter swept from the room.

'Why, going to Sam, of course,' she replied, as though the answer were obvious.

'I think life might have been easier if we'd had sons,' her father observed as she slammed the door behind her. 'I feel very old,' he complained to his wife.

'Dr Lacey?'

Hand outstretched, she went forward. Bless Adam, she thought; he's come up trumps again.

'Fred Bohman.' Her hand was pumped enthusiastically. Dr Bohman was a large man, with a girth that she couldn't have spanned with both arms. 'This is kinda unorthodox,' he went on, looking her up and down. 'You *are* a doctor?'

'Cross my heart,' she assured him solemnly. She still couldn't believe she'd got here so quickly. It was mostly thanks to Adam. When she'd rung him to say she wouldn't be coming into work, he'd somehow wangled her intentions out of her. He hadn't tried to dissuade her or even complained at being let down. Instead, he'd rung back half an hour later, having got her a cancellation place on the next flight to New York. She'd had to arrange the internal flight connection herself.

'You do realise how tight the security is going to be in the hospital?' Fred Bohman asked.

She hadn't, until Adam had pointed it out. When he'd casually mentioned he knew a medical administrator at the hospital Sam's son had been transferred to, she hadn't been able to believe her luck.

'I can get you in, Dr Lacey,' Fred Bohman told her as he led the way across the car park. 'But after that you're on your own.'

She nodded. Adam had said as much. 'What'll you do if he has you thrown out on your ear, Lindy?' he'd asked.

'I don't know.'

Adam hadn't appeared to find anything to criticise in this fly-by-the-seat-of-your-pants policy, or, if he had, he'd kept quiet about it.

There was an obvious media presence on the steps in front of the building, but once inside the building the security measures were less noticeable. Nobody stopped her as she walked beside the authoritative bulk of Fred Bohman.

'You'd be amazed how many crazy people will do almost anything to see Sam Rourke,' Fred observed, with a shake of his head. 'The guy's sitting at a deathbed and someone actually asked him for an autograph. And a reporter who got in nearly left through the window.'

Lindy saw the sign for ITU and her palpitations got worse. She swallowed convulsively, but there was nothing to lubricate her throat and her mouth was bone-dry.

'ITU's straight ahead.'

'Thanks; I'm very grateful.'

'Give my best to Adam. The family will be in the relatives' lounge, or with the boy.'

What the hell are you doing, Lindy? she asked herself as she walked forward. She pulled out the stethoscope she'd shoved into her pocket and looped it around her neck to add a little authenticity. They can't really arrest me for impersonating a doctor when I am one—can they? she thought. The window-dressing might distract attention from the sign she felt sure was plastered across her forehead, saying 'INTRUDER'.

The door was ajar and with a nudge of her hip it swung inwards. What am I going to say? What am I going to do? she wondered. In the grip of a gut instinct that was stronger than anything she'd ever encountered in her life, Lindy hadn't permitted herself to think beyond this point.

I'm probably the last person he wants to see, she thought as she stepped forward into the room. Deep-pile carpet and easy chairs set in informal groups around the room gave no indication of the tears that had been shed within these four walls. She'd had to break bad news to relatives often enough to know that there was no easy way to do it, no setting that made it easier.

He wasn't there. She blinked and inhaled deeply. There were two people sitting at the other end of the room. They sat in chairs placed opposite one another, their knees touching. The man held the woman's hands between his. Lindy could see the tension and weariness from where she stood.

'I...I'm sorry, I'm intruding.'

'You're a doctor?' The woman got to her feet. Her pretty face was white and strained; dark shadows filled the hollows beneath her eyes. 'Is it Ben?'

This was the mother of Sam's child. 'I don't work here,' Lindy admitted. She had been willing to do almost anything in her desire to see Sam, but she couldn't lie to these people. 'You must be Marilyn. I'm a...I'm a friend of Sam's. I hoped I might be able to help.'

'He's sitting with Ben.'

'I'm sorry...I shouldn't be here,' she faltered. It was a mistake—this woman's grief made her reasons for being here seem petty. It put her own suffering into perspective. She turned to go, but the other woman caught her arm.

'No, don't go. Sam needs someone here. I've got Murray. I think I'd be insane by now if he wasn't here. We didn't think Sam had anyone.'

'It's not like that. We're not...'

Ben's mother had a lovely smile; when it wasn't

tinged with sadness it must have made her quite beautiful. 'You came; that must mean something.'

The quiet words stilled Lindy's panic, but not the doom-laden certainty that she'd made a big mistake coming here. It means I'm a fool, a lovesick clown, she silently replied. Sam doesn't want to see me. He can't stand the sight of me!

'Perhaps I could leave a message for Sam?' she suggested. Yes, a message would be much more sensible—safer. 'I don't actually know where I'm staying yet.' She reached in her pocket for the address of the hotel Adam had suggested.

'He's conscious.'

Lindy started at the sound of Sam's voice. She was pushed to one side as Marilyn surged forward. The woman flung her arms around Sam's neck.

'Thank God, thank God!' she kept saying, over and over.

Her husband, a tall, slim man with a shock of auburn hair and a thin, intense face, touched her arm. She released Sam and buried her face in her husband's shoulder.

'You go in; I'll wait here,' Sam said.

The couple didn't need a second bidding. Sam watched them go with an expression of yearning on his face. His throat worked hard, and as he turned she could see the unhealthy grey tinge of his skin. He didn't appear to see her as he lowered himself stiffly into a chair. He closed his eyes and his head drooped forward.

Lindy's professional eyes could see he was close to collapse, but his incredible will was driving him on. He was keeping everything inside and it was destroying him.

'Hello, Sam.' She came to sit beside him.

His head came up and he looked at her without any

sign of recognition. There was neither rejection nor pleasure in his eyes. 'Rosalind? Ben's awake.'

'That's marvellous.' There was a lump of emotion in her throat. She wanted to hold him, but she knew he was deliberately holding onto his rigid control. 'I spoke to Marilyn; she's lovely.'

'Yes,' he replied vaguely. He brushed a weary hand across his forehead. The line between his brows deepened. 'What are you doing here, Rosalind?'

'I wanted to help.' She was frightened for him; he looked so close to the edge.

He just nodded, and she wasn't even sure he'd heard her. 'Where are you going, Sam?' She got to her feet, too.

'It's time for me to go.'

'Aren't you going back in to see Ben?' she asked gently.

'He wants his mom and dad,' he told her, without any inflection in his voice. 'He didn't know who I was, Rosalind.' His voice was harsh.

The pain behind that simple statement made her heart ache. Feeling helpless, she instinctively reached for his hand. Her own was instantly enfolded in a fierce grip.

'Where are you staying, Sam?'

'I came straight here.'

'When was that?'

'Tuesday…no, Monday. Straight from Hong Kong. We were spying the lie of the land for our next project.'

She did some mental arithmetic—four days, the flight from Hong Kong…God knew when he'd last slept. 'And have you slept at all?'

Sam looked impatient and shook his head.

'Have you eaten?'

'I've had coffee.'

No wonder he looked like death. It was surprising he was still on his feet. 'Wait here, Sam; there's something

I have to do. Don't go anywhere until I come back.' To
her relief he didn't query her instructions. Exhausted, he
slumped back into a chair.

Lindy found the nurses' station. 'Could you page Dr
Bohman for me?'

The administrator didn't keep her waiting long.

'I'll have a cab waiting at the exit for you.' He handed
over the security card that unlocked the staff entrance.
'There shouldn't be any press hanging around that side
of the building.' He glanced at the gold watch on his
wrist. 'Is that all now? Because...'

Lindy planted a kiss on his cheek. He looked startled
and pleased. 'That's it, I promise,' she told him. 'And
bless you.'

Sam didn't evince much interest as Lindy led him out
of the building, after first leaving the contact number of
the hotel Adam had given her at the nurses' station.

She gave the name of the hotel to the cab driver. She
sighed with relief as they were whisked through the hospital gates without incident.

Lindy sat and watched whilst Sam ate the food she'd
ordered from Room Service. Before he'd finished eating
his head fell back and he was instantly asleep, as only
the very young or the completely exhausted could. I love
him so much it hurts, she thought as she watched him.
In sleep he had a touchingly defenceless look. She
couldn't fool herself that that would last.

She'd appeared when Sam had pushed himself beyond
the boundaries of physical and mental endurance. When
he woke up he'd be the Sam of old and nobody, least
of all her, was going to lead him anywhere! She wasn't
complaining—she'd wanted to help and, in a small way,
she had by being in the right place at the right time.

No, her lack of trust had ruined anything they might
have had together. Knowing she'd let the past ruin what
could have been a golden future left a bitter taste in her

mouth. If she'd ever needed proof that Sam was a loving
father, she certainly had it now. If only she'd been capable of faith...

The sound of his regular breathing didn't alter as she
removed his shoes and placed the quilt from the bed over
him. She didn't bother unpacking her small overnight
bag. There wasn't much point. It didn't contain anything
much beyond the barest essentials. With one last look at
his sleeping face she lowered the lights and climbed into
the double bed alone.

A muffled curse and a clatter woke her in the early hours
of the morning. 'Sam?' Still half asleep, she switched
on the bedside lamp.

Sam was standing at the far side of the room. He'd
knocked over a small table. He blinked in the sudden
light. 'What the hell? *Rosalind?*' Incredulously, he
turned towards her. Seeing the wariness slip into his
eyes, she could have wept. 'Where am I?'

'Don't you remember?'

'Ben did wake up? That wasn't a dream?'

'No, that wasn't a dream.' She levered herself up on
her elbow and adjusted the neckline of her baggy nightshirt back over her shoulder.

A deep sigh of relief lifted his big chest and she could
see the ripple of muscles through the thin wool of his
knitted shirt.

'What time is it?' He looked at the face of his wristwatch. 'Why did you let me sleep this long?' He scowled
as he reached for the phone.

'I left the number by the phone.' The hospital was his
first thought, as she'd known it would be.

Sam picked up the piece of paper and flicked her a
quick glance before he addressed himself to the task in
hand.

'He's asleep,' he said a few minutes later. The tension

was still in him, but it was under control now. 'They don't give much away.'

'Was he badly injured?'

Sam shot her a surprised look. 'You don't know?'

What could she say? That she'd just jumped on a plane without even being aware of the full facts?

'Not really.'

His eyes were narrowed speculatively, but he replied readily enough. 'He got hit by a drunk driver.' The viciousness in his eyes made Lindy shiver. He looked capable of wringing the life out of the criminal fool. The empathic link between them made her ache.

'Multiple injuries, internal bleeding and a fractured skull. They say they'll let me know if there's any change overnight. Now, do you mind filling me in on a few facts? Just how the hell do I happen to be in a hotel bedroom with you?'

That was the one question she'd been dreading. 'They only had one room left.' She tried to quell the blind spurt of panic as he came over and sat on the side of the bed.

'We'll get to the sleeping arrangements in a minute,' he promised. 'I mean, how did I get here?'

'In a taxi.' It was a compromise. 'I led you by the hand' might provoke an explosive reaction.

'God, yes, I remember now.' He shook his head, as if to clear a fog. 'How did you happen to be in the States, Rosalind?'

'I had a meeting...with Dr Bohman, the medical administrator,' she improvised wildly. Well, I can't tell him the truth, can I? she thought, justifying this detour from fact. 'I wanted to widen my horizons—professionally speaking, that is.'

'How providential.' She couldn't tell from his expression if he believed her or not.

'I thought I'd look you up.'

'It would seem you've done a bit more than that.'

'I'd have done the same for anyone.'

'Is that a fact?'

His scepticism made her pluck fretfully at the sheet. 'You were nearly dead on your feet.'

'That was your professional diagnosis, was it?'

'The fact is, Sam, you may like to think you're super-human, but you're just like the rest of us—you need food and sleep. You won't be much good to your son unless you take care of yourself.'

'You took care of me,' he said softly. His glance moved to the chair with the crumpled quilt and to the half-eaten food on the tray.

'As I said, I'd do the same for anyone.'

'Doesn't your boyfriend object to your missions of mercy?'

'Boyfriend? What? Oh, yes…no. That is… What are you doing?' she asked in alarm as he peeled off his shirt.

'I don't usually sleep fully clothed.' His jeans slid to the floor and he lifted the corner of the quilt. 'How far are you prepared to go with this comfort thing?'

'Sam, don't be an idiot.' She tried to sound as if this was all some silly joke. The hard, hair-roughened thigh that came to rest against her own was no joke. The com-bination of desire and fear that swirled through her veins was a heady cocktail.

'If I slept in that chair tonight I *would* be an idiot.' He calmly lay back on the pillow that still bore the im-pression of her head. Chancing a look into his vivid eyes, she saw he wasn't calm—anything but!

'You'd be a gentleman.' She gave a startled cry as he reached out and yanked her down beside him.

'Something nobody has ever accused me of.' Several days' growth of beard on his jaw gave him a look of dangerous dissipation.

'That's nothing to be proud of.' It was desperately hard to speak when he was stroking the side of her face.

'You smell so good.' He inhaled deeply. 'Hell, I don't suppose *I* do. I can't recall when I last had a shower. I must be pretty ripe.'

Now was the time to agree with him and tip him out of her bed. It was a heaven-sent opportunity and she neatly side-stepped it. 'No, you smell marvellous,' she told him honestly. He did—spicy, masculine and musky.

Sam's smile was filled with satisfaction. He rolled onto one hip and reached out for her. His fingers curved possessively around the slim curve of her upper thigh. 'I need to forget.' His eyes met hers and there was a plea for understanding there.

'I know,' she murmured. Forget about protecting yourself, Lindy, she thought, silently giving herself permission to do what instinct told her was the right thing. She took his face between her hands and kissed him. His lips parted on a sigh and they strained against one another as they each drank deeply—hungrily.

He didn't have to be afraid she'd think tonight was the start of something. She knew this was a unique situation and she just happened to be there. Sam was reaching out. He needed an outlet, a release from the unbearable pressures of the past days. For a man used to making things happen, the awful feeling of impotence must have been hard to bear.

She wouldn't refuse him anything he needed. This was her chance—probably the only chance she'd ever have—to physically express her love for him.

'Tell me what you need, Sam.' She pressed herself sensuously closer to the warmth of his body. 'Let me make you feel good.' Her arms slipped around his neck and her fingers stroked the tight, bunched muscles of his shoulders.

He took a deep, sharp breath. 'Are you for real?' he grated hoarsely. His eyes smouldered as he nuzzled the corner of her mouth.

'Don't I feel real?'

'Let's just check on that one.' His hands moved under the light nightshirt she wore, travelling over the smooth, rounded contours of her buttocks. 'That butt feels authentic to me. I'd be willing to stake my reputation that you're no dream.'

'I had a dream,' she whispered softly. She dropped her head to run her tongue over the flesh of his chest. It tasted salty. 'Only I hadn't fallen asleep at the time,' she reflected out loud. 'I dreamt I woke up and you were in bed with me. You didn't have any clothes on; neither did I.'

'That's called a fantasy, not a dream, Rosalind.' He lifted the nightshirt over her head and she pressed the pointed tips of her breasts against his chest. A deep, voluptuous sigh of pleasure shuddered through her. Her knees locked at either side of his muscular waist and she slowly ground her hips against him. His arousal dug into the softness of her belly.

'Have you any idea what you're doing to me?' he demanded hoarsely.

She lifted her head and smiled slowly at him. Her hand slid lower down his body, and paused. 'I've got a fairly good idea.'

His body shuddered with tension and he pulsed against her hand. 'Witch,' he gasped throatily.

'I just want to make you feel good, Sam,' she purred. Legs straddling his body, she ran her fingers over his torso in slow, rhythmic strokes. She couldn't tear her eyes from the receptive quiver of muscles under her fingers. She tangled her fingers in the short, dark hair on his chest.

'You make me feel crazy!' he growled.

She gave a grunt of surprise as she found herself flat on her back with his heavy body pressing her into the mattress. His glance was hot and taut as it skimmed over her flushed, aroused features. Panting hard, he took her hands in his and, interlacing his fingers with hers, placed them at either side of her flushed face.

There was no subtlety in his kiss. It was rough and needy, and it ripped a series of soft moans from her throat. 'You can't escape me!' he whispered.

'Did I give you the impression I wanted to?' She looked at him through half-closed eyes. Her breasts, flushed rosy, rose in time to her short, shallow inhalations.

Sam made a terrific effort to retain control, but as he sank into her and felt her hotly close around him he became oblivious to anything but the desperate, blind need that drove him.

'Did I hurt you?'

Lindy looked up, startled, and belted the thick unisex robe around her waist. 'I didn't know you were awake.'

'Did I?'

She blushed, the memory of his lovemaking just as vivid as the imprints left on her body this morning.

'You were very energetic for a man on the edge of exhaustion.' She tried to hit just the right note, not too light, not too intense. She couldn't tell him the experience had shaken her profoundly. She couldn't tell him she'd discovered an aspect to her character she hadn't even suspected existed.

'Should I apologise?'

She couldn't be that cool! 'That would spoil it.'

He relaxed slightly, and she realised for the first time that he'd been awaiting her reply tensely. He sat up and the covers slipped down to his waist, revealing his torso. Dry-throated, she averted her eyes. She could exactly recall the satiny texture of his skin beneath the light dusting of dark hair.

'I have to go to the hospital.'

That was it. It was over. She had steeled herself for this moment.

'Will you come with me?'

The words robbed her of composure. 'Me?'

'The medics might be more forthcoming with you. It's incredibly frustrating when they're obviously holding back. I don't want to be humoured, I want the whole truth. But if you're busy...?'

'No!' She took a deep breath and excised the fervour from her voice. 'I've nothing on today.' Her shrug was casualness personified. So, he didn't need her to share his burden—but he did need her, and that was better than nothing.

'Thanks.' Totally lacking self-consciousness, he lifted the covers and stood up.

The pattern on the carpet really was very interesting, almost hypnotic, Lindy mused.

'Have you showered?' he asked.

'Yes.'

'Pity.'

Coward that she was, she didn't look up. It was truly pathetic, she reflected, how powerfully the husky suggestiveness in his voice could arouse her. She continued to lay out her clothes.

'Where's your luggage?'

She mentally backtracked, trying to recall exactly what she had said to him. God, my memory's not good enough for this lying lark, she thought anxiously.

'It was lost...at the airport.' She was so pleased with this lie she felt inspired to embroider it slightly. 'It went to Hawaii.' She looked up and her self-confident smile faltered. 'Will you put some clothes on?' she snapped. How was a person supposed to lie convincingly when faced with that sort of distraction?

'I got the impression you liked my body last night.'

'That's below the belt.'

A smile quivered on his lips. 'Wasn't that your specialist subject?'

'Sam!'

'All right, all right, is this better?' He folded a bath towel around his middle. 'Did you wear this for your meeting with the medical administrator?' He picked up the navy cotton striped top that matched the navy canvas trousers she'd travelled in yesterday.

'It was a casual meeting.'

'It must have been. Anyway, I'm in a similar situation to you; I've nothing to wear.' He regarded the clothes that hadn't been off his back for almost a week with disfavour. 'I'll ring down to Reception and get some things sent up.'

'The boutiques in the foyer won't be open yet.'

'Then they can open early,' Sam replied. 'I think you'll find they'll be flexible.'

This statement proved accurate. A selection of items appeared whilst Sam was still in the shower.

'Anything to suit?' he asked as he walked in towelling his dark hair vigorously.

'Plenty,' she observed drily. She frowned at yet another designer label. 'How did you know my size?' Even the lingerie, which made her mouth water, was an exact fit.

Sam cupped one hand. 'Thirty-four C,' he said, squinting at his approximation.

'That ability must come in very useful!' she commented with a flush.

'It does,' he confirmed. 'Keep anything you like and I'll send the rejects back.'

'I can't afford these,' she observed regretfully.

'Who's asking you to pay?'

'I can't accept clothes from you.'

'Why not?'

'It wouldn't be...it wouldn't be appropriate.'

'You can owe me.' His voice suggested the subject was beginning to bore him.

Of course, he's got more important things to think about than what knickers I wear, she thought guiltily. She selected a pair of tailored cream linen trousers and a striped silk shirt.

'I'll pay you back.'

He looked impatient, but didn't argue the point. He *was* impatient, but she managed to persuade him to eat breakfast before they left for the hospital.

Marilyn didn't appear surprised at her presence. She nodded in recognition as Lindy walked in beside Sam. As she listened to the attending doctor's assessment, Lindy's heart sank. The impressive list of injuries were not in themselves life-threatening. The scans showed there had been no permanent brain damage, but...

'What are you trying to say?' Sam brusquely halted the meandering commentary littered with technical jargon.

'He's saying the kidney damage is permanent, Sam.'

The doctor shot her a surprised glance. 'You're a doctor?'

Lindy nodded. Sam hadn't flinched, but his jaw tightened and he looked to the medic for confirmation.

'Is Lindy right?'

'I'm afraid so.'

Marilyn let out an anguished moan and flung herself into her husband's arms. 'My poor baby,' she sobbed.

'What exactly does this mean?' Sam persisted.

'The boy will need to be on dialysis for the rest of his life.'

'What about a transplant?'

'That is, of course, an option, but a suitable donor doesn't always come up overnight. We have tissue-typed

Benjamin, of course...a close relative would be best...
A sibling?'

'I'm pregnant.' Marilyn wiped the tears from her face.
'Does that rule me out?'

'Honey...' Her husband drew her closer to his side.

Sam looked with surprise from one to the other. 'Congratulations. That leaves me.'

Lindy flinched, even though she'd known he was going to say it. This was the man she accused of being an
unnatural father!

'There's no guarantee you'll be compatible, Mr
Rourke.'

'Do what you have to do.'

'We can arrange counselling if the tests prove...'

'I don't want counselling. I want you to get on with
your job.'

'We wouldn't contemplate surgery until the boy's recovered from his other injuries.' That said, the doctor
retreated tactfully.

'Oh, Sam, how can you ever forgive us?'

'There's nothing to forgive, Marilyn.'

Lindy would have retreated herself if Sam hadn't been
blocking the doorway. She felt like an interloper. This
was a private moment and she had no place here.

'We had no right to ask you not to see Ben. We should
have told him you were his father. I played on your guilt
deliberately.' The admission made Marilyn's eyes fill
with tears. 'It wasn't fair to you or Ben. It was selfish.
When I saw you sitting at his bedside, I knew I'd been
wicked.'

'You were only doing what you thought best, love,'
her husband said comfortingly.

'Not best for Ben,' his wife wailed. 'You have every
right to feel bitter. You were always a good father.'

'An absent father,' Sam reminded her.

'That wasn't your choice. You went where the money

was. You gave up your college education for us, Ben and I. You made sure I finished my education, and how do I repay you?' The tears started again.

'There's no point in rehashing the past, Marilyn. The only thing that matters now is Ben.'

The doctor reappeared in the doorway. 'Mrs Tenant, your son is awake. He's asking for you.'

'My face—do I look all right? I don't want him to know I've been crying.'

'You look fine, honey.' Murray turned back as they followed the white-uniformed figure. 'Come with us, Sam.' Awkwardly, he tried to bridge the gap.

Sam shook his head. 'Not now.'

Lindy was choked with emotion. When she thought of the things she'd accused him of, when all along... She'd known for some time that she'd been wrong, but the extent of his sacrifices made her feel wretched. Wretched but proud.

'Why don't you go with them?'

'The boy doesn't want to see a stranger. He wants his mom and dad.'

How that matter-of-fact statement must have hurt. Lindy curled her fingers into fists to stop herself from reaching out to comfort him. That wordless gesture would have implied an intimacy which, despite the wild passions of the night, didn't exist between them. Lindy had no illusions about what last night had meant to him. For her, it belonged in the small collection of special memories she'd keep fresh for ever in the years ahead. Memories of Sam that no one could take from her.

'Tell me about transplants, Rosalind.'

'First of all they'll see if you're compatible. The better the match, the more likely the transplant will be successful. They'll want to find out if you've got two healthy kidneys before they do anything. All surgery carries a risk, Sam.' Sounding objective was one of the hardest things she'd ever had to do. She felt sick with apprehension at the risk he was taking, but she knew her instincts were purely selfish.

'There's a chance of rejection?'

'Yes, but I'm no expert. I don't know the up-to-date statistics. As I said, the better the match, the more the likelihood of success. You have to remember that you'll only have one kidney, though.'

'You only need one, right?'

'If you're involved in an accident that injures the remaining kidney, you're going to find yourself in a similar situation to Ben.'

He made a dismissive gesture. 'It's possible I can *do* something. Do you know what a relief that is? Have you any idea how frustrating it's been the last few days sitting there, helpless to do anything, watching him slipping further away?'

His clenched fists ground into the muscles of his thigh. 'He looked so young. I kept thinking, Why? Why Ben? What had he done to deserve that? Why wasn't it me lying there? If that bastard who did it had been in the same room, I'd have killed him.' His eyes, filled with dark torment, touched her face. 'Seriously, Rosalind, I wanted to smash something. I've never considered myself to be a violent man...'

The depth of his emotion hit her like a tidal wave. 'I'm only playing devil's advocate, Sam.' His pain squeezed her heart like a vice, but what could she say? He didn't need platitudes. 'The medical staff here are honour-bound to point out all the pitfalls. They'll tell you the same thing I have, but in more detail.'

'I understand.' He took a shuddering breath. 'Thanks, Rosalind; thanks for everything.'

My exit line, she thought. 'I'll leave you to it, then,' she said brightly.

'To what?'

Don't be awkward, Sam, she silently prayed. This is hard enough as it is.

'Dr Lacey—Rosalind—I hoped I'd find you here.'

'Sam, this is Dr Bohman.'

'Pleased to meet you, Mr Rourke.' Fred Bohman pumped Sam's hand. 'Sorry to hear about your son. I wondered, Rosalind, if you'd pass this on to your brother-in-law when you see him. It's a copy of the snap I took when we were in Geneva last year. I promised him a copy.'

'Of course; no problem.' She smiled as he rushed on his way.

Sam looked over her shoulder at the photo, which showed a row of men each with a glass in his hand. Adam was in the centre of the shot, carrying a silver statuette.

If she knew Adam the prestigious award for medical research was probably stowed in a dark cupboard somewhere, which was where this photo was likely to be stowed too, she thought with a wry smile.

'That's your brother-in-law?' Sam placed a shapely, blunt-ended finger on the spot where Adam smiled back at the camera.

Lindy snatched the photo away. She hadn't even been aware that he was looking over her shoulder. 'Yes, that's Adam,' she confirmed.

'Good-looking guy.'

Perhaps he hadn't noticed. 'Anna thinks so,' she responded carefully.

'Then he's not your boyfriend?'

It had been too much to hope for. 'Obviously not.' If he tries to suggest that I'll sock him, so help me... she thought.

He didn't try to take a rise after all. 'That figures.'

'It does?' she responded, seriously worried by the expression on his face.

'You didn't come here to see Bohman, did you, Rosalind?'

'Not directly, but he was very helpful.' She managed a good example of her very best cool, professional smile.

'Why did you come here?'

Even though the air-conditioning was a little on the cool side she was sweating.

'You just happened to be passing?'

She gasped. That was plain cruel. He knew; she could see it in his eyes. But he wasn't going to be satisfied until she admitted it.

'I saw the headlines about Ben and I thought...'

'You thought?' he prompted.

'I thought you might need my help.' It sounded feeble, and she knew it.

'So you hopped on the first plane,' he deduced. 'Wasn't that taking good neighbourliness to extremes?'

He was taunting her and she didn't deserve that! So he was still mad with her for not trusting him, but this wasn't fair. She placed her hands on her hips and eyed him belligerently.

'I came because I had to. Because I love you!' she declared. 'Satisfied?' Tears trembled on her eyelashes.

CHAPTER NINE

'NOT nearly satisfied,' said Sam.

'What do you want—blood?' Lindy burst out.

'Only a little bit, but if this is a bad time I can come back.' The impatient incomprehension on Sam's face made the young medic wish himself elsewhere.

They'd been so immersed that neither of them had noticed the white-coated figure enter the room.

'No, no, that'll be fine.' Sam played the perfect patient flawlessly as he swiftly soothed the apprehensive doctor. He rolled up his sleeve.

Lindy bit her lip; the urge to giggle obviously stemmed from hysteria. Under the circumstances humour was wildly inappropriate.

'Do you happen to know what blood group you are?'

'AB negative. Is that good?'

'It's rare.' The white coated young man admitted. 'And it's the same as Ben's, which is a start. You won't feel a thing.' The platitude brought an ironic smile to Sam's lips. 'There. All finished.'

'He looked about sixteen,' Sam commented as he rolled down his shirt-sleeve once the medic had departed. 'Hell, that's one of those things I always swore I'd never say when I was a kid.'

'Our own expectations are usually the hardest to live up to.'

'So you love me, then?'

Lindy cast him a wary look. He sounded as though he was discussing the weather. 'This is no joke.' It was callous of him to derive pleasure from her misery. Was

163

that pleasure she read on his face? It was hard to interpret the flare of emotion in his eyes.

'It'd better not be.'

This ambiguous statement didn't give her any further
insight into his reaction to her declaration. At least he
hadn't laughed or looked triumphant. Perhaps the way
she'd treated him no longer seemed particularly important, considering what he'd been through the last few
days. Slipping down his list of priorities gave her little
comfort. At least when he hated me he was thinking
about me, she mused. The sheer perversity of this
thought made her frown.

'You needn't worry that I'm going to read too much
into last night,' she reassured him. 'I know the circumstances were exceptional.' She knew his passionate intensity had been a form of release from the unbearable
tension he'd been under. Perhaps friendship could be
salvaged from this mess?

'You feel you were some sort of passive receptacle
providentially sent to liberate my pent-up emotions?'
The flicker this time was quite definitely anger.
'Strange,' he said softly. 'You didn't give the impression
of passivity.' She squirmed under his relentless scrutiny.
'The last time I had unprotected sex a baby was con-
ceived.'

'Me too,' she responded faintly. It was a bolt out of
the blue. Why didn't I think of that? she asked herself
incredulously. Her knees showed an alarming tendency
to buckle and she slid into a chair.

'I thought it might be something like that,' he mused
openly.

Lindy stared at him with horror. It had just slipped
out in the shock of facing a complication that she honestly hadn't even considered. Why had she needed him
to alert her to the possible consequences of last night?
It *should* have been the first thing she'd thought

about. What *had* been the first thing that had occurred to her this morning? She gave a tiny groan—she'd been too busy keeping her hands off Sam's sleeping form to be able to think anything, barring how glorious he looked and how good it was to wake up cradled in his arms.

'You couldn't possibly know.' She dragged a trembling hand through her soft hair.

'As you didn't see fit to confide in me, no. I only had vague suspicions.'

'The way *you* confided in me about Ben?'

'I would have if you'd given me the chance,' he reminded her grimly. 'You didn't trust me,' he added tautly.

'There were reasons why I—' She broke off and buried her face in her hands. 'It's too late now. I know you'll never forgive me.'

'Did you forgive me for accusing you of talking to the gutter press about Ben?'

'You know I didn't do that?' She gave a smile of sheer relief. 'I'm so glad.'

'You were right, it was Magda. She's a crazy, screwed-up female and I was a mug to give her a job,' he said bluntly.

'It's a pity nobody saw fit to warn me about her.'

With an inclination of his head, Sam acknowledged this. 'Her husband's a nice guy; I've worked with him several times. A while back she had a drug problem and with his help she kicked it. Tom asked me to keep an eye on her while he was away working. Like a fool I said yes. She turned up on my doorstep one night with some story about a guy stalking her. If I'd known at the time she had a history of inventing that kind of thing I'd have saved myself a whole lot of grief, but I was sucked in.

'I took her along to the police and they seemed pretty

casual about the whole thing, which, given her history, wasn't surprising. She seemed so terrified I let her stay a couple of nights, until Tom got back. She had some lame excuse when I caught her going through my desk, and I started to realise she wasn't all she seemed. She'd read a whole bunch of letters I'd kept from Marilyn and found photos of Ben. She gave me her word that she'd never breathe a word and, after a few tense months, I didn't give it any more thought. Fortunately, Tom believed me when I denied I'd been sleeping with her.'

'She told him that!'

'What, no lynch mob?' he taunted wearily.

Lindy coloured. She deserved that. 'No.' Her trust had come tragically late. She could now see that Sam Rourke was one of the most honest, decent men she had come across—or ever would. The words 'honest' and 'decent' had an old-fashioned ring to them, but they suited him. He was no saint to be put on a pedestal, but that wasn't what she wanted. If she hadn't allowed the past to haunt her, she might have been more objective when Magda had made her accusations. Things might have been very different.

'The fact she wasn't the only house guest I had at the time helped,' Sam continued. 'Besides, people—present company excepted—find my sincerity irresistible.'

The self-derisive twist of his lips made her wince. 'It was Tom who asked me to consider her for the job this time. He said she'd been in therapy and was completely rehabilitated. When he found the cheque she'd got from the paper he managed to squeeze the truth from her. He got straight on the phone to me. Poor guy...' He shook his head pityingly. 'He was devastated, but he'll stand by her. At least until she lets him down the next time.'

'Why?' Lindy asked wonderingly.

'He loves her.'

The intensity of his stare made her shiver. Was there

a message in those blue eyes, or was it just her over-
active imagination at work?

'Incidentally, I managed to ruin that little rat reporter's exclusive,' he told her with grim satisfaction.

'How did you do that?'

'I advised Marilyn to give the story to a reputable rag
and to beat the worm to the punchline. She was reluctant,
but at least she had control over what they printed. These
people are experts at presenting the truth in a distorted
fashion. Not an ideal situation, but the best I could do
under the circumstances. It limited the damage, but fate
stepped in and kept us in the news,' he observed wryly.
'If I hadn't been such a mug about Magda, none of this
would have happened.'

'She's obsessed with you,' Lindy told him reluctantly.
Magda was the last person she wanted to talk about. 'She
goes around telling everyone that you were lovers. If
only I hadn't listened to her.' Her eyes were dark with
misery. 'It looks like she fooled us both.'

'There, you just did it, didn't you?' He saw her blank
look of incomprehension. 'You just forgave me.' He pa-
tiently spelt out his meaning. 'Do you think so badly of
me that you can't credit me with the same ability,
Rosalind? Or is it yourself you're so unwilling to forgive? You're an expert at punishing yourself.'

'I've had a lot of practice,' she replied slowly. His
words subtly shifted her perception. Do I think, deep
down, I'm not worthy of happiness? she pondered. It
was an unsettling thought.

'Sam.'

Marilyn and Murray had come quietly into the room.

Sam shot to his feet. 'Is something wrong?' The colour drained from his face and fear was stark in his eyes.
A fear he'd grown used to living with over the past few
days.

'No, no...' Murray soothed hastily. 'Ben would like

to meet you.' He looked to his wife for support, and she nodded encouragingly back.

Lindy knew she would never forget the uncertain longing on Sam's face. The torment in his eyes etched itself indelibly on her mind.

'I don't want to intrude.'

Sam had his emotions firmly back in place. But the fact that he was a stranger, that he needed an invitation to see his own son, stirred all the buried anger and resentment he felt. He had done what was in his son's best interests, but he hadn't liked it. Inside, he'd raged against the injustice of it. Despite what Marilyn implied in her present emotional state, she was no angel. If—no, *when*—Ben got back to normal, she'd soon revert back to her old ways.

'We've told him, Sam,' Marilyn said tentatively, holding out her hand. Sam stared at the 'olive branch' blankly, as if he didn't understand what she was saying. 'We told him you're his natural father. He knows you wanted to see him. He knows about the financial support,' she said awkwardly. 'And the trust fund you set up.'

'You shouldn't have done that, Marilyn.' His fingers briefly touched hers before falling to his side. 'It'll only confuse the boy.'

Murray laughed. 'You don't know Ben.'

'No, I don't.' A nerve in Sam's lean cheek throbbed.

There was a difficult silence which Marilyn filled. 'He's resilient, Sam, a real fighter. Nothing fazes him. Don't underestimate him. He doesn't know about his kidneys yet. We thought we'd wait until you have your test results back.'

Sam nodded and took a deep breath. 'Are you sure about this?' He quashed the cynical thought that this was some reward for offering his kidney to his son. It wasn't as if they could retract it if the test results were negative— They *can't* be, he thought.

'Very sure.'

'Rosalind?'

Lindy stared at his hand. He wants me, she thought. Deep satisfaction flared in her heart. Now wasn't the time to ponder the significance of the gesture.

Fingers entwined with his, she followed him into the white, impersonal atmosphere of the intensive care unit.

She hadn't expected the resemblance. The same colouring, the same blue eyes. It was startling.

'He's easily tired, Mr Rourke.' The nurse looked pretty enough to be in a soap.

'Fine.' Lindy could feel the coiled tension in Sam's body. His face looked gaunt, and possibly rather daunting to a young child. She needn't have worried as she watched the discipline of an actor come into play and the hard lines of tension melt away. His shirt might be sticking to his back and his palms might be slick with sweat, but no casual observer would have guessed this was a moment he'd dreamed about for years.

Only Lindy wasn't a casual observer. Let it go well for him, she silently prayed. I can't bear it if he's hurt again!

'So you're my father.' His voice held caution and curiosity, but no trauma. Lindy felt Sam relax fractionally. 'What do I call you?' She heard the challenge in the young voice. Sam must have heard it too, though he gave no indication.

'My friends call me Sam.'

'Is she your wife?'

'I'm not married.'

'Then I haven't got any brothers or sisters?' There was a wistfulness in the youthful voice.

'Not yet.'

At first Lindy thought Sam was referring to Marilyn,

but then, from his expression, she swiftly saw the reference was much more personal. She felt the colour rise up her neck until her face was on fire. Sam regarded the Technicolor treat with interest. A low chuckle from the bed averted her attention. The miniature version of Sam was looking from her to Sam with a very grown-up expression on his face.

'I wouldn't mind a brother or even a sister. I don't think Mom can have any more children.'

'That's a shame,' Sam replied. It wasn't his place to dispel this misconception.

'You're an actor?' Sam nodded. 'I want a proper job…' The provocation was deliberate. Ben waited for his words to have some effect.

'Very wise,' Sam approved. 'Did you have something particular in mind?'

'A doctor, I think.' He looked at the various selection of tubes attached to his pitifully thin frame. 'It seems pretty cool.'

'Rosalind's a doctor.'

'Cool!' She'd obviously just shot up in his estimation. 'I nearly died, you know,' he told her with the ghoulish relish common to the young and very old.

'We know.' Lindy shot Sam an anxious look, but beyond flinching he didn't react.

'Do you cut dead people up?'

'Only living ones.'

'Cool!'

The nurse came back into the room. 'I think our patient could do with some rest now.'

Lindy's nose twitched and she cynically wondered if the nurse reapplied Shalimar for all the visitors.

'Fine, Nurse,' Sam replied.

'You can come back if you like.' The offer was issued in a gruff, offhand manner.

Sam stared at the thin white hand; an intravenous line

poked out of it, stretching the resilient childish flesh. The expression in his eyes was shaded by the sweep of his dark lashes. Lindy blinked back emotional tears as she watched them formally shake hands. The strength of Sam's big, capable hands somehow emphasised the fragility of the child.

'I'd like that,' Sam replied in an equally casual manner.

Back in the corridor he leant heavily against the wall. He held out his hand and looked at it incredulously. 'I'm shaking,' he said slowly. 'I'm actually shaking. Give me a room full of movie moguls out to axe my latest film any day. I was terrified of saying the wrong thing.'

Lindy was moved by his candour. 'You didn't,' she assured him. How did I ever think this man was shallow and insincere? she wondered with amazement.

His brooding gaze shifted to her face and the eagerness in his expression made her want to take his beloved face between her hands and kiss his doubts away.

'It's a start, isn't it? He's cautious...'

'That's natural enough,' she said earnestly. 'You're not the only one feeling your way, Sam.'

'He liked you.'

'I liked him,' she said huskily. How could she fail to like anyone who reminded her so poignantly of the man she loved? Sam's expression was making her skin tingle with that familiar, dangerous electrical surge.

'Our conversation was just getting interesting when we were interrupted.'

Lindy sighed. She'd been wondering when he was going to remember that. 'I don't think there's much point in raking over all that.'

'Don't you?' he grated. 'Well, I do.' He grabbed her by the arm. 'Not in here,' he said, looking around the corridor with distaste. 'I've hated hospitals, ever since Dad died.' He shuddered. 'I want the sky over my head.'

A fine sentiment, but does he have to drag me along like a sack of potatoes? God knows what people are thinking, she thought, smiling with some embarrassment at a group of nurses who turned and stopped to stare at the spectacle she and Sam presented.

'Sam, really, you can't behave in this . . . this Neanderthal manner.'

'Regression is a very liberating experience.'

She twisted her wrist but his fingers were like a manacle. 'I'm sure bank robbers say the same.'

'I have no intention of robbing a bank.'

Cold comfort, but what *was* his intention? She didn't have much opportunity to ponder this question; she was too busy keeping up with his long-legged lope.

'Not that way, Sam!' she cried in panic as she realised the direction he was taking. 'The press!' she wailed—too late.

Five minutes later, feeling as though she'd been through a rugby scrum, she sat back in a cab and glared at Sam resentfully.

'You did that on purpose!' she accused. 'You could have avoided them. I feel...' She shuddered.

'Soiled?' he suggested enigmatically.

'If you knew that,' she whispered incredulously, 'why...? Were you trying to punish me?'

'Don't start that again,' he replied, a shadow of anger crossing his face. 'It's a lot like falling off a horse. The longer you take before you get back on, the worse it gets. Do you think you're unique? Do you think I like people rifling through my garbage? I cope and you can cope.'

There was a ruthless gleam of determination in his eyes. 'If they think you're giving them what they want they back off just enough to give you room to manoeuvre. If you hide behind a ten-foot-high electric fence they'll move heaven and earth to find what you're hiding. It's a balancing act, and I'm good at it—trust me!' It was an order, not an invitation.

'But I don't need any lessons in handling the media,' she told him, bewilderment in her eyes. 'They're not interested in junior doctors—unless we manage to kill off a patient.' Her only claim to fame had been her association with Sam, and that was about to end.

'They'll be interested in my wife.'

Fortunately, she was already sitting down. For one brief, glorious second she thought he meant he loved her. Then reality stepped in and the explanation for his extraordinary statement presented itself. The anticlimax made her want to weep.

She might be pregnant, and after Ben he wasn't taking any chances. Sam wasn't going to lose his child a second time. She'd seen his paternal instincts at work, and she wasn't about to underestimate them.

'Oh, no!' she groaned, closing her eyes. The cab came to a halt.

'I'm impressed by how well you're managing to restrain your delight.' He paid off the cab driver and waited stiffly for her to get out of the vehicle. Lindy cast a swift sideways look at his face. Remote but determined just about covered it.

This was going to be a very painful process. She was about to refuse something she wanted more than anything in the world. She didn't want to marry Sam for the sake of a baby, even if it did exist. If she couldn't have his love, she didn't want anything.

They walked in silence for a few minutes. A jogger, recognising Sam, produced a pen and asked him to sign her hand.

'I'll never wash again!' she declared as she ran off.

The words made Lindy recall that she been strangely reluctant to step under the shower earlier that day. She hadn't wanted to wash away the scent of Sam that had lingered on her skin.

'The chances of my being pregnant are slim,' Lindy said, pausing beneath a beech tree. He mustn't see how badly I want to go along with this idea, she thought. 'I know you think you're super-fertile…' The light laugh went completely wrong.

She caught a leaf and began rubbing off the greenery with her thumb to expose the delicate skeleton. Then, experiencing a pang of regret that she'd thoughtlessly destroyed something beautiful, she crumpled it in her hand and dropped it on the ground.

'It's happened to you before, though. You had a child?'

She looked up sharply. 'You want to know about that?' His expression was impossible to read.

'It seemed you wanted to tell me earlier. You have chapter and verse on my developing years…'

'That's a bit of an exaggeration, Sam.'

'What's wrong, Rosalind? Don't you trust me with your secrets?'

He had her there. 'There's not a lot to tell.' She gave a shrug. 'A fairly common, if sordid, tale.' She couldn't prevent the bitterness creeping into her voice. 'I went to medical school at eighteen, and to say I was green would be understating the case. He was my personal tutor. You could say he took his task a little too literally.'

Now it was hard to see what had attracted her. He'd been a man of the world in her young eyes—sophisticated, worldly.

'I found out he was married when I told him about the baby. He already had children.' She swallowed to clear her throat. 'He became…' Her expression grew distant. 'He was angry. He asked me if I could prove it was his.'

A spasm moved Sam's lips and his hands clenched into fists. 'The child?'

It was hard to meet his peculiarly intense gaze. She swallowed again and shook her head.

'You had a termination?'

'No!' she denied fiercely. 'That was what Paul told me to do. He even offered to pay,' she told him bleakly. 'No, I lost the baby early on. It all happened so quickly, Mum and Dad never even knew. Anna was in London—she was a dancer then. She looked after me and later Hope came.' A shudder rippled through her body.

'You thought I was like that bastard?' The anger in his voice made her tense.

She knew it must seem the greatest insult imaginable to him. Knowing now what sort of man Sam was, she could well appreciate his outrage.

'You have to understand, Sam, I haven't been able to trust my judgement since then.' Her voice trembled with the intensity of her feelings. 'When you didn't deny Magda's lies, I felt as if the same thing was happening all over again. The things I said to you were all the things I'd wished over the years I had said to Paul. I didn't say anything, you see, when he said all those vile things to me. I just stood there. I should have defended myself, but I was paralysed. I'd been so frightened when I found out about the baby, but I kept telling myself that Paul would make it all right.'

Her mouth twisted in a self-derisive smile. 'I really believed he would. I'm truly sorry I used you to purge myself of old demons, Sam. You deserve better.'

'I've got broad shoulders.'

He did—he had broad shoulders and eyes filled with suppressed anger. 'Were there many other men...before me?' Her expression answered him and he turned his face away, but not before she'd glimpsed the agonised expression there.

'It's not that hard to substitute work for...' She broke off. She couldn't really say any more without revealing the true extent of her feelings for him. Sam had stirred her sexuality, a part of her that had lain dormant over the years.

'You were seduced by a bastard who abused his position of trust,' he said in a savage voice. 'What the hell have you got to be ashamed about, woman? Why are you so eaten up with guilt?'

Her face crumpled and she turned away, pressing her cheek into the bark of the tree. Sam caught her by the shoulders and inexorably turned her around. A firm hand on her jaw tilted her face up towards him.

'It's my fault I lost the baby. I didn't want it. I was afraid it would remind me of Paul and I hated him. I wanted to lose it. It was my fault.' The words spilled out of her and her voice rose with each successive syllable.

She fatalistically waited for the disgust, the distaste. She'd never longed for any man's approval the way she did Sam's, and now he would despise her.

She was jerked roughly into his arms, until her head collided with the solid surface of his chest. Strong arms anchored her next to his heart. She continued to gulp in air, trying desperately to silence the sobs that racked her body.

'Hush, baby, don't cry. It's all right,' he crooned softly in her ear. 'A person is judged by their actions, Rosalind, not by their fears and thoughts. Hell, we'd all be clapped up in jail if that were the case. Your reaction was a natural one—one you'd have worked your way through eventually if you'd had the opportunity—if the child had lived.'

'I know that,' Lindy sniffed. She rubbed her cheek

against the soft fabric of his shirt. Knowing it was irrational didn't stop her *feeling*. 'Do you think I haven't told myself that? Afterwards I knew that deep down I had wanted the baby, but it was too late. On the surface I could be logical about it, but underneath... God, I've got your shirt all wet.'

She lifted her head and dabbed ineffectually at the fabric. Her wet eyelashes fluttered upwards and she looked uncertainly into his face. 'I really *did* want that baby, Sam.' Her face puckered into a vehement frown.

'There'll be other babies.' With infinite tenderness he brushed the strands of soft hair from her face.

Her fraught nerves were tranquillised by the warm, mellow sound of his voice. His reassurance made her glow with relief. He understood, he hadn't condemned her. Why did she always sell him short?

'No!' Suddenly, with all her strength, she pushed him away. What a fool I am! Just because the man's kind and sensitive it doesn't mean he loves you. He only wants you because you might be the mother of his child, a voice inside her cried. Her whole being rebelled against settling for that—she *couldn't* settle for that!

Sam staggered backwards several steps before he regained his balance. 'What the hell...?'

'I'm not going to marry you,' she said, with an obstinate expression on her tear-stained face.

'You said you loved me.'

'You have to rub it in, don't you?' She scrubbed the back of her hand over her face to blot the last of the dampness.

'I'm trying to be patient here, Rosalind.' He pressed his steepled fingers together until the knuckles turned white. 'You can't tell me you don't care for me enough to marry me. You dropped everything and leapt on a plane for me when you didn't even know what sort of reception you'd get. Is it marriage that you object to? Do you prefer us to live together? Talk to me!'

Was he deliberately being obtuse? she wondered. It wasn't what she said that was the issue; it was what *he* had very noticeably *not* said!

'What are you going to do, Sam?' she asked bitterly. 'Cancel the ceremony if I'm not pregnant?'

'What has you being pregnant got to do with it?'

His incomprehension seemed genuine. 'Just about everything,' she replied indignantly.

'Explain yourself!' His temper wasn't just frayed at the edges, it was unravelling completely, if the expression on his face was anything to go by.

'It's perfectly understandable that you don't want the same situation to arise as it did with Ben,' she said reasonably. 'You don't have to worry—I'd never try to stop you having access to your child. Though all this is a case of putting the cart before the horse...' Her voice trailed off. He didn't look reassured—he looked explosive! 'If you stop to consider this quietly and calmly you'll see that marriage is a wild overreaction to the situation.'

'Quietly and calmly?' he thundered, in a voice that made the birds in the topmost branches of the tree flutter away with an alarmed series of squawks. 'I could strangle you.' Lindy closed her eyes as his dark face came closer. His hands came to rest at either side of her face against the tree trunk.

'Are you all right, lady?'

'Is this guy bothering you?'

Recalling the lectures about crime and violence she'd received from all her friends and relations when they'd first heard she was going to America, on another occasion Lindy would have given these two a wide berth. 'You could be murdered in broad daylight while people walk past' had been a favourite homily.

Her two knights wore not shining armour but trainers and baseball caps. A person shouldn't be cynical, she decided.

'She's fine,' Sam snapped.

'Who asked you?' Despite the aggression, her saviours took an involuntary step back as Sam straightened up to his full height. Lindy didn't blame them; he looked quite capable of—well, anything!

'I'm fine, boys…' She stopped worriedly. Did you call young men like this boys without giving insult?

They looked frankly relieved, though sceptical at her reassurance. 'We could call a cop.' They regarded Sam with open suspicion.

Lindy shook her head. 'Don't worry, I'll be fine,' she said heartily.

They continued to look suspiciously back over their shoulders as they strolled away.

'Didn't that guy look like Sam Rourke?'

'Sam Rourke's short in real life; I read it somewhere,' came the scoffing retort. 'Besides, can you see Sam Rourke going anywhere without a bodyguard?'

'Probably his hairdresser, too…' Their laughter faded into the distance.

'That was so sweet. It restores my faith in human nature.'

'Sure,' Sam drawled. 'It makes me go warm and mushy.'

'There's no need to be sarcastic.'

'There's no point in trying to change the subject, Rosalind.'

'The subject was closed.'

'You think,' he responded silkily.

'This has been a very stressful few days for you,' she said kindly. 'You're not in the best state, emotionally, to be making big decisions.'

'You'd like me to propose to you unemotionally?'

'I thought that was what you did.' She compressed her lips to hide the tremor.

'For God's sake, woman, you know I'm in love with you!' For once, his beautifully mellow voice sounded hoarse.

'I know what?' she yelped. She couldn't believe what she was hearing.

Sam stared at her incredulously. 'Of course I love you! I *told* you I loved you,' he reminded her from between gritted teeth.

'That was before...before I said all those vicious things. You acted like you hated me,' she protested faintly. This could just be a very realistic dream. She pinched herself just to be on the safe side—it hurt!

'Sure, I thought I hated you, or at least I wanted to—that was the hell of it—I couldn't! I've been through weeks of undiluted purgatory because I love you. Do you think I'm going to stand here and let you tell me not to be emotional about it?' he yelled. 'Why the hell do you think I want to marry you?' He took a long, slow look at the stricken expression on her face. 'You thought it was just because of the baby, didn't you?' he accused her hoarsely.

'I was only putting two and two together,' she faltered. Sam loves me—he does! She felt peculiarly light-headed. I'll never, ever be cynical about happy endings in my life, she vowed. Joy was beginning to get the better of the strange, numb feeling.

'I'll buy you a calculator and you have to promise me never, *ever* to attempt mathematical calculations in your head again. I thought *you* hated *me* until you turned up here. I can't tell you what it meant to me that you did that.' Emotion throbbed in his rich voice. 'If I had any nagging doubts that you'd do something like that out of friendship, they were dispelled after last night.' He laughed at the shyness in her flushed face. 'It was pretty wild, wasn't it?'

'Oh, Sam!' she cried, with a catch in her voice. 'Oh, Sam.' She knew she was in danger of sounding repetitive, but it was all she was capable of saying.

'Kiss her!' a loud voice suggested.

There was a huge roar of approval. 'Yeah, kiss her.'

Sam didn't even turn around, but he was never one to disappoint an audience. He swept Lindy into his arms in a masterful fashion and the applause was loud.

Bemused but smiling, Lindy gasped for breath once her feet touched the ground once more.

'That's so romantic. Want some popcorn?' Misty eyes were dabbed.

'Yeah, thanks.' A boy on roller-blades dug deep.

'Sam...' Lindy stood on tiptoe and peeped over his shoulder.

'Uh-huh...?' he said, his voice muffled against the skin of her throat.

'There are people...people watching us.' At least twenty people of both genders and various sizes were gathered in a half circle.

'I know.'

'You know!' she burst out indignantly. 'God, but you're such an exhibitionist,' she accused hotly. 'How can you share a precious, private moment...? Mmm...' Her words were lost in the warm recess of his mouth.

'Now I call *that* a kiss,' a female voice sighed.

'Way to go!' someone whooped.

Lindy was relieved when even Sam decided that enough was enough. He led her through the gathered throng amidst comments that made her blush deepen. To her indignation, he even stopped to sign a few autographs.

'What can I say?' he responded when she complained.

'I'm a performer. However, I think we should go somewhere we can't be disturbed—urgently.'

'That's a relief,' she mumbled. If I could only bottle
this feeling. I don't want to forget a single second, she
thought fiercely. 'This might seem pushy, but we do
have a perfectly good hotel room,' she reminded him.

'Excellent! I like pushy,' he approved. He paused in
the act of flagging down a taxi. 'What hotel was that,
incidentally?' he said casually.

Lindy grinned and told him.

'It's easy to say "Let's get married",' Lindy said a little
later, sitting on the edge of the bed.

'Speak for yourself,' Sam retorted. The bed swayed
gently as he joined her. 'You didn't do the asking. Neither were you very co-operative.'

'I mean, it's a lovely idea, but you've got to be practical.'

Sam heaved a sigh and continued to loosen his tie. 'It
was only a matter of time, I suppose. A more sensitive
soul might be a bit upset about your lack of enthusiasm.'

'How can you say that? I was enthusiastic in the taxi,
wasn't I?' She blushed deeply at the answering gleam
in his eyes.

'I thought it wiser to distract you before you started
getting logical on me,' he replied glibly. 'Ouch!' he
complained, falling back onto the bed with her on top
of him. The humour suddenly evaporated from his face.
'God, but I love you!'

'I still don't quite believe this is happening, Sam.'

'I love these wispy bits around your face,' Sam continued, winding one strand of hair carefully around his
finger.

Lindy reached down to touch his face and his lips
closed over one finger. She let out a soft cry as he began
to suckle softly. He only stopped to turn over her hand

and place his mouth against her palm. Heat pooled like liquid in the pit of her belly.

'I can't think when you do that.'

'I should hope not,' Sam growled, with a lecherous grin. He deftly pulled her down beside him and, turning his body, looped one leg over hers. His muscular thigh effectively pinned her to the bed. 'Hush, my love.' He touched a finger to her lips. 'I know you want to talk about the conflicts of our careers, but all that's just so much detail. We can cope with details later. The important thing is we love one another. You do love me, don't you?'

'Do you need me to tell you?'

'Every second of the day,' he confirmed.

'I love you, Sam Rourke, for ever!' she declared solemnly.

'When I came to England, I was determined to see you suffer. I felt so betrayed when I thought you'd gone to the press. Then I saw you come out of the hospital. Did you know that skirt you were wearing is transparent in some lights?' he teased, but his eyes held the dark memory of deep pain. 'I knew I loved you, no matter what you'd done. Then *he* joined you.'

'Adam,' she prompted tenderly, when his voice became suspended by pain.

'Yeah, only I didn't know who he was. I wanted to kill him for touching you, and you didn't even seem to mind.'

'We're a tactile sort of family, Sam.' She stroked his cheek to prove the point. 'It was Adam who got me on the plane here. I wasn't capable of anything once I got this idea into my head that you needed me. I was like a homing pigeon and you,' she said, half-shyly, 'were my home.'

'And you're mine,' he responded fervently. 'And talking of families... About Ben; it's something I have to do.'

'I know that. It's just if I ever lost you, Sam...' The impossible horror of the idea darkened her eyes.

'You won't,' he vowed. 'I promise.'

'I trust you.' She knew Sam understood the significance of this statement.

'I know,' he replied simply.

EPILOGUE

LINDY watched the boy and man emerge from the water. They shook their heads like two otters and the drops of salt water gleamed in the sun like diamonds.

The boy, a tall, skinny child with legs like a young colt and arresting blue eyes, reached her first. Panting, he peeled off the snorkel and mask and flopped down beside her on the hot sand.

'It's terrific,' he said, rolling onto his stomach. 'Why don't you try? He's not a bad teacher.'

'I find him a bit bossy,' Lindy confided. She knew how precious this time together was to Sam. She tried not to be obvious about it, but it was important to give father and son time alone. She had the rest of her life with Sam—why be greedy?

'I heard that.'

'You were meant to.' A warm, intimate smile reached her eyes as Sam lowered his rangy frame down beside her.

'Cover up, Ben,' she advised, squinting up at the sun. She passed him a vivid, printed shirt.

'Yes, Doc,' he responded with a grin.

'Bossy, the woman said!' Sam teased.

'You too,' she said sternly. She had already slipped a loose shirt over her bikini. The shade from the palm-leafed parasol dappled Sam's brown chest and shoulders with a chequered pattern. She wanted to reach out and touch the satiny, oiled smoothness of his skin. Then do it! an inner voice urged her. A smile of fierce exhilaration spread over her features. I can—I'm allowed to! she realised wonderingly.

185

'You look like the cat that got the cream,' Sam observed. He gasped as her cool palm touched his midriff.

A gold ring gleamed on her right hand; it was plainer than the sapphire and diamond cluster she now sported on her left hand, but just as precious to her. She'd had the gold cuff-link she'd carried around with her during the wilderness weeks turned into a ring. She intended to wear it always to remind her of how lucky she was.

'I'd purr if I could.'

'You can.' His deep voice held laughter.

Lindy shot him a warning glance and inclined her head towards the boy.

'If you two are going to start all that mushy stuff, I'm off. I'm going to get one of those ice-cream things with pineapple and chocolate and cream. Do you want one?'

'No!' the adults replied in unison. The amount one thirteen-year-old boy could consume had reduced them to silent awe on more than one occasion over the past week.

'I think that child's thirteen going on thirty sometimes,' Sam mused.

Lindy flopped back beside him and watched Ben's skinny legs retreat up the beach. 'I wonder where he puts it?' She placed a hand on her still flat middle. 'If I ate half as much as him I'd be the size of a house.'

'A sexy house.'

'Don't try and butter me up.' She wiggled her hips to carve her behind a deeper hollow in the soft sand as Sam placed his hand over her bare belly.

'It's hard to imagine this one will ever be that size.'

'Sometimes it's hard to imagine this one is really there.'

'You saw the scan.'

She gave a deep sigh of pleasure. 'I did.' It had been one of those precious moments that she'd look back on over the years, a memory she'd polish and keep fresh, and she knew Sam felt the same way.

'Do you think your parents suspected when we insisted on an early wedding?' Sam asked curiously.

'Probably, but they're far too tactful to say anything. I expect they probably think a man who takes his son on a honeymoon, especially when the honeymoon precedes the wedding, is capable of anything!'

'This isn't your honeymoon, woman.' Sam rolled onto his belly and there was warm promise in his eyes. 'I'm going to introduce you properly to the other woman in my life on your honeymoon. Don't worry, I won't have you climbing the rigging in your present condition—light duties only. Seriously, though, love, you didn't mind about Ben coming, did you?'

Lindy's warm smile banished the anxiety from his eyes. 'Don't be daft!' she advised briskly. Her fingers ran lovingly down the strong curve of his back. When they encountered the raised ridge of a recent scar, her brow puckered.

There had been anxious days after the operation had taken place. Happily, the outcome had been all anyone could wish for. Ben had a new lease of life and Sam had recovered from the major surgery remarkably swiftly. Despite the fact they were here in the Caribbean to convalesce, she had to remind Sam he was meant to be taking things easily. In fact at bedtime she had to be pretty stern and take things into her own hands!

When the Tenants had allowed Ben to come along, it had been a sign of the altered relationship between Sam and his son. Marilyn seemed to feel less threatened by Sam's involvement in the child's life, though caution still existed on both sides. Watching the warmth between father and son develop from tentative beginnings, Lindy had felt privileged.

'You're blushing!' Sam exclaimed.

'I'm not! Don't tickle; that's not fair!' she gasped as she tried to squirm free of his hands.

'Not until you tell me what you're thinking about.'

'All right, all right, stop it—please.' Breathless, she subsided. 'If you must know, I was thinking about last night.'

'You have a very creative streak. I'm not easily shocked but—' He broke off, laughing deeply at her affronted expression.

'You snake, Sam Rourke!'

Sam caught her flailing fists. 'Be gentle, I'm a weak man,' he chided.

'You're a sinful man,' she responded, meeting the wicked glitter of his azure eyes.

'Do you mind?'

She didn't; she didn't mind in the least.

Mother's Day is Around the Corner...
Give the gift that celebrates Life and Love!

Show Mom you care by presenting her with a one-year subscription to:

HARLEQUIN
WORLD'S BEST

Romances

For only $4.96—
That's **75% off the cover price.**

This easy-to-carry, compact magazine delivers 4 exciting romance stories by some of the very best romance authors in the world.

Plus each issue features personal moments with the authors, author biographies, a crossword puzzle and more...

A one-year subscription includes 6 issues full of love, romance and excitement to warm the heart.

To send a gift subscription, write the recipient's name and address on the coupon below, enclose a check for $4.96 and mail it today. In a few weeks, we will send you an acknowledgment letter and a special postcard so you can notify this lucky person that a fabulous gift is on the way!

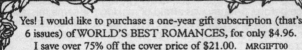

Coming Next Month

HARLEQUIN PRESENTS®

THE BEST HAS JUST GOTTEN BETTER!

#2097 THE MARRIAGE DEAL Helen Bianchin
When Michael Lanier had made his wife choose between her career and their marriage, she'd left him. Now Sandrine's career was facing a crisis, and only Michael could help her. He would do so, but for a price: Sandrine must agree to share his bed and his life once more!

#2098 THEIR ENGAGEMENT IS ANNOUNCED Carole Mortimer
To avoid his mother's matchmaking, Griffin Sinclair had announced that he was going to marry Dora Baxter. She had to play along—but it wasn't going to be easy, as Dora had secretly been in love with Griffin for years....

#2099 AUNT LUCY'S LOVER Miranda Lee
In order to gain her inheritance, Jessica had to live in her aunt Lucy's house for a month with Sebastian—described in Lucy's will as her "loyal and loving companion." But could this blond hunk really have been her aunt's *lover*?

#2100 EMERALD FIRE Sandra Marton
Having fallen for Slade McClintoch's powers of seduction once before, Brionny was afraid of making the same mistake again. And she couldn't be sure if he was really interested in her, or if he was simply trying to discover her precious secret....

#2101 THE UNEXPECTED WEDDING GIFT Catherine Spencer
Ben Carreras is astounded when an old flame gate-crashes his wedding insisting he's the father of the baby boy in her arms and that he must take his son. But how can Ben break this bombshell to his new bride...?

#2102 A HUSBAND'S VENDETTA Sara Wood
Although Luc Maccari's marriage to Ellen had been blistered with passion, she'd abandoned him when he needed her most. Now Ellen was back, and Luc wanted revenge. But seducing Ellen reminded him of what he'd been missing, too—and then he discovered her heartrending secret....

CNM0400